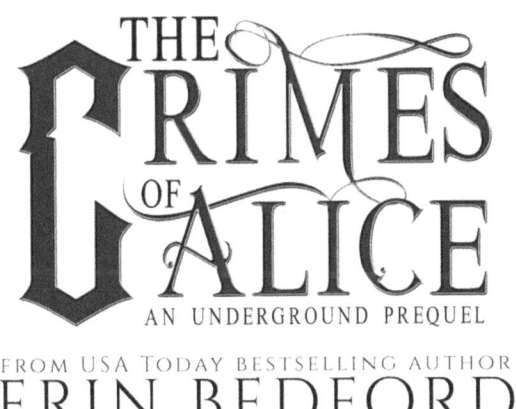

THE CRIMES OF ALICE

OF

AN UNDERGROUND PREQUEL

FROM USA TODAY BESTSELLING AUTHOR

ERIN BEDFORD

The Crimes of Alice © 2018 Embrace the Fantasy Publishing, LLC

Also by Erin Bedford

Curse of the Fairy Tales
Rapunzel Untamed
Rapunzel Unveiled

Her Angels
Heaven's Embrace
Heaven's A Beach
Heaven's Most Wanted

Academy of Witches
Witching On A Star
As You Witch
Witch You Were Here

Granting Her Wish
Vampire CEO

THE CRIMES OF ALICE

AN UNDERGROUND PREQUEL

CHAPTER I

IT ALL BEGAN WITH a game of bridge. A frightfully exasperating game which I had no honest interest in playing, but it was the only respectable form of entertainment one could find on a Sunday afternoon.

"Your draw, Alice." My younger sister, Violet, tapped her cards on the table in front of her, her lips pursed with displeasure. She wasn't any happier to be playing the game than me. In fact, the way she kept flickering her eyes toward Edmond, one of our brother Fredrick's friends, Violet would much rather be kissing the roguish young man. Scandalous, for sure.

"Alice," Violet said my name again. This time, it held a hint of impatience. "Alice!"

"Violet," our mother chastised from her seat a few tables over in the game parlor. "Do not raise your voice to your sister."

Violet scowled. "She's got her head in the clouds again. No doubt dreaming about that place. That Won—"

"Violet." The sharp tone of our mother's voice caused Violet's lips to clamp shut. "Now, where were we?" She smiled politely at her companion, Mister Carroll, who had just come back to town from Cheshire, England.

He was handsome enough with a straight nose and a pleasant smile. He wasn't balding or overweight. It helped that he had a job even if it was in a bank. Though, from my mother's point of view, that was far better than any of the other attributes.

"I believe you were telling me about the accomplishments of your eldest daughter, Rhoda," he said, "in an effort to have me take her as my wife."

A giggle escaped me. I quickly covered my mouth with my hand, but my mother caught it. She sent a warning glare my way before giving Mister Carroll a coy smile.

"Now, Mister Carroll, you spoil the fun of matchmaking. You know with my children grown, that is all I have left that brings me joy."

Mister Carroll caught me looking and winked before replying, "Is that all? Then I must do my best to make sure you do not pass without finding such enjoyment. It is my responsibility as a gentleman." He lifted his cup of tea to his lips, taking a long drink before sitting it back on the saucer.

A sharp pain in my calf made me cry out. My eyes jumped to my sister who sat with a smug grin on her lips. "What was that for?"

Smiling behind her cards, Violet flickered her eyes to Mister Carroll. "You know."

Wrinkling my nose at her, I drew my cards and discarded two. "Your turn." I tried to pay attention to the game, but then it was my name on Mister Carroll's lips.

"And what of Miss Alice?"

I forced myself to stay in my seat, my eyes on my cards though I barely even saw the hearts or spades in my hand.

"Oh, Alice?" My mother chuckled nervously, the way she always did when any young gentleman showed any interest in me. It wasn't that I was ugly by any means. In fact, out of all my sisters, I have been told on many occasions to be the fairer one. However, my mother called me a unique being, but what she really means was that I was mad, quite bonkers, gone 'round the bend. Any of them would do to describe me in her eyes.

"Yes." Mister Carroll crossed one leg over the other, his hands sitting in his lap. "I find her quite delightful, and she is the more beautiful of your daughters."

I couldn't help but smirk at my mother's discomfort. Ever since our father passed, she had been bound and determined to have us girls married off. Fredrick was a kind enough brother and keeper, but soon he'd have his own wife and then children to go along. He couldn't take care of three spinster daughters and his widowed mother on his paltry professor's salary.

Violet wouldn't be too difficult to marry off. She was pretty and had a bubbly personality. If only she could mind her manners better... though I was sure she could say the same about me.

Rhoda was a different story entirely. Stern and studious, she had no time for silliness or the like. Some called her too serious. I called her my best friend. She was the only one of my family besides father who didn't think I was mad, that the dreams I had weren't delusions, or that I needed to be sent away. It was her that had fought to keep me at home, or I'd have been sent to the sanitarium already.

I glanced over at Rhoda, who gave me an encouraging smile over her book. She was well over twenty and didn't care a lick about what anyone thought. She would never need a man to make her happy or find her way. Out of us three, she was the most adventurous and the most well to do.

Me, on the other hand, well, I'd be stupid to not take any hand that was offered to me. If Mister Carroll wished to marry me, then I couldn't very well say no. It was either him or the asylum, and gray was not my color.

That is what prompted me to lay my cards down on the table, muttering a firm, "I fold," before standing from my seat and, without invitation, taking the seat between my mother and Mister Carroll.

"I do believe someone called my name. I'm Alice." I held my hand out to Mister Carroll who shook it with a bemused twinkle in his eyes.

"It is a pleasure to meet you, Miss Alice." Mister Carroll brought my hand up to his mouth, pressing his lips to the knuckles. A light flutter filled my stomach but was replaced by another sharp pain on my thigh.

My eyes moved to my mother and her offending fingers which had just left my lap. Her brows were drawn tight and her mouth set in a thin line. I was messing up her plans.

"Mister Carroll will be at the game hall this evening, so you need to be on your best behavior," she had told us. "Do not call attention to yourselves. Rhoda, wear the green gown and I better not see you reading. Men do not take kindly to women who know too much." Rhoda had rolled her eyes at mother at the time and, based on the fact that she had not waited more than five minutes before pulling her book out, never intended to go along with mother's plan.

Apparently, neither did I.

"Mother," I cooed, sliding my arm through hers and smiling softly toward Mister Carroll, "you never told me Mister Carroll was so handsome. And here you were going to give him to Rhoda." I leaned forward and brought my hand up as if to tell him a secret, and he moved toward my hand conspiratorially. "The only item she finds remotely interesting is a dead piece of wood covered in ink."

Mister Carroll threw his head back and laughed. "Well, I do enjoy a good book myself, but real life is much more interesting, don't you agree?"

I opened my mouth to agree, but Violet said, "If you had dreams like Alice, then nothing in life is real."

I glared at my sister, who only stared me down before turning back to her cards. To Mister Carroll, I said, "One cannot control what they dream any more than they can decide if they will breathe."

"Too true," my mother concurred and tapped the table with her knuckles.

"Very well said." Mister Carroll nodded. "And what kind of dreams do you have Miss Alice?"

I shifted in my seat, unsure if I should really reveal what it was that ran through my head each night, if I should tell of the terrible and wonderful adventures I had ever since the tender age of ten. I, myself, didn't know where they came from. An overactive imagination? Some kind of childhood trauma that had morphed into dreams so that I might cope with whatever had happened?

The child version of myself used to insist they were real, that everything I'd seen and experienced had actually happened.

However, as I grew older, my stories became less entertaining and more upsetting to those around me. No one wanted to hear about a rabbit in a waistcoat or a big blue caterpillar who smoked a hookah pipe and talked in circles. If I had dared even to mutter a trace of evidence of being given drugged tea by a handsome stranger with a top hat, they

13

would have for sure have sent me on my way by now, marked as damaged goods and too scandalous for marriage.

I didn't know whether it was something in Mister Carroll's eyes, the sincerity of his question, or maybe it had nothing to do with Mister Carroll at all, and I was just tired of pretending. Whatever might have happened to be the reason, I didn't have a moment to contemplate it before I spoke.

"Have you ever been to Wonderland, Mister Carroll?"

"Wonderland?" He sat back in his chair, adjusting the jacket of his suit, a real keen interest in his face. My mother made a noise to interrupt us, but she must have seen something too because, for once, she did not rebuke my words and insist I was only teasing.

Eager for an open ear, I leaned forward in my seat. "Yes, Wonderland. A place where everything is backward and nothing it what it seems."

Mister Carroll let out a laugh. "Oh, you must mean the higher offices of the political court. I have found myself falling into their rabbit hole of lies and mischief a time or two though I find it surprising for a young lady such as yourself to be so interested in politics."

I smiled politely, shaking my head. "No, not politics, though rabbit holes are quite a way to travel. I talk of talking animals and cats with smiling faces. Fairies and mad tea parties. The likes of things you have never dreamed of before."

And from there, I went on and on, regaling Mister Carroll with my dreams of Wonderland. The more I talked to him, the more interested Mister Carroll became, so much so that my mother eventually had to pull me away from him because of the late hour.

"Miss Alice?" Mister Carroll called after me as we made our way to the gaming hall door.

"Yes?" I paused between my sisters, my brother having had taken my mother to our carriage already.

"May I call on you? I would be delighted to hear more about this Wonderland."

"You would?" I pursed my lips, waiting for him to call it all a jest.

Mister Carroll stood from his seat and approached us, my sisters twittering to each other behind me. Stopping before me, he took my hand in his and held it.

"You have made a very dull evening, a delight. I would love nothing more than to look upon your face and hear about your wonderful tales. As long as you do not bring up banking ledgers, I could listen to you talk for the rest of my life." He brought my hand up to his mouth, brushing his lips against my knuckles.

My sisters gasped and then giggled behind their hands before Rhoda shooed Violet out the door giving me a meaningful look. I could hear her words in my head as plain as if they had been said from her mouth. *Do not mess this up.*

I wouldn't have another chance like this, maybe ever.

Despite the apprehension in my heart, I nodded. "I would be delighted, Mister Carroll."

A joyous smile curled up Mister Carroll's lips. "Please, call me Lewis."

CHAPTER

I WOULD HAVE LOVED to say our relationship blossomed into a glorious love affair. That each day was like a blessing and we would go on long walks and gaze lovingly into each other's eyes.

Love. A four-letter word that one could only hope to find in friends and family. Any expectations of it in a relationship, especially with my reputation, was utter nonsense.

"I'm quite surprised you were able to catch such a fine man," Violet commented as she primped in the mirror for the fifth time in the last twenty minutes. "How did you dazzle Mister Carroll into marrying you?"

I sniffed and rolled my eyes, thankful that my mother was greeting the guests, so she couldn't chastise me for it. "I did nothing of the sort. Lewis is too smart for those kinds of games." I adjusted the skirt of my wedding dress, trying to soothe my jittery hands.

"Well, you must have done something right," Violet continued, coming to stand beside me in the full-length mirror. "No man would go to all this trouble to marry someone as odd as you for no reason. He's even paying for the wedding." She played with the gemstones embedded in my pale blue gown. "You should have let him buy your dress. Then at least maybe it would be more in fashion."

I pulled my arm away from her with a frown, fluffing my underskirts and adjusting my veil over my blonde curls. "There's nothing wrong with my dress, and I don't need fancy things to make me happy."

"But they don't hurt." Violet smirked, primping her hair now in my mirror. "You could have at least gotten a white dress like Queen Victoria. You know, it is the height of fashion now."

Rhoda, who had been quietly sitting in the corner a book in her hand, snorted. "How impractical. A white dress. You might as well throw a bucket of mud on it and be done with it."

"Agreed." I peered over my shoulder at my eldest sister, and we wrinkled our nose at each other with a grin. To my younger sister,

18

I said, "Unless you plan to catch a wealthy man, you might as well get thoughts of a white wedding dress out of your mind."

Violet pouted, but it didn't last long. Her fits never did before she was off daydreaming about some other impossible thing. And they call me the odd one.

At least, that was one thing I didn't have to worry about. Lewis loved my stories of Wonderland and prodded me daily for more information. I almost felt as though he had an obsession with it, even more so than I did.

Nevertheless, it had gained me a husband, and I would soon be out of my brother's home and no longer a bother to anyone. I hummed to myself, thinking of all the different changes I could make to my new home. Lewis had given me permission to redecorate the whole estate if I wished.

"Whatever your heart desires," he had said, kissing my cheek. That had made my heart flutter and my palms sweat. At least, I knew that we wouldn't have any issues in the boudoir.

A knock came to the bedroom door and interrupted my thoughts. Frederick's dark head peeked into the room, and his eyes scanned around before landing on me. A small smile graced his lips as he pushed the door open completely.

"Alice, aren't you a vision!" He opened his arms as he came to me, and we hugged briefly. Pulling back, he frowned. "You know you really should have gone with white or even a cream color. You are going to be a wealthy woman now."

"See?" Violet pointed a finger at me.

Pushing away from Fredrick, I adjusted the high collar of my light blue gown. "I don't want a white dress, and besides, blue was father's favorite color."

At the mention of father, the room grew quiet. A pensive expression crossed Fredrick's face before he spoke. "You're right, blue is perfect. Isn't it, Violet?"

"Yes. Quite." She nodded vigorously, her eyes brimming with tears. She sniffed and turned her face. "Excuse me for a moment."

I watched quietly as she left the room and then sighed.

"Getting anxious?" Fredrick asked, brushing my hair away from my face.

I bobbed my head.

"Do not worry yourself," he continued. "In half an hour, you'll be going down the aisle with yours truly at your arm, and then a brief time after, you'll be Misses Lewis Carroll."

His words were supposed to comfort me, but they only made my anxiety heighten. I hadn't told anyone, I wouldn't dare. I barely even had the courage to admit it to myself, but I wasn't even sure I wanted to be Misses Lewis Carroll. I would no longer be known as Alice Liddell and would always be referred to as Lewis's wife. The very thought of it made my breath quicken.

"Are you alright?" my brother asked, concern coloring his face.

I nodded but didn't speak. I couldn't find the air to.

"She's going to faint," Rhoda announced, rushing to my side. "Let's get her to the window. She needs fresh air."

The two of them took me by the arms and helped me to a seat near the window, opening it up so that the warm August air poured inside. Rhoda stood behind me, smoothing a hand over my back in slow circles.

"That's it. Slow deep breaths. You'll be alright."

I did as she directed, staring hard at the floor beds outside the window. The wedding was being held on Lewis's estate which had a massive garden in the back. I had mentioned a wondrous flower garden I had seen in Wonderland once to Lewis, and he insisted we have one just like it for our wedding.

I should be grateful, but at that moment, all I could think of was the suffocating pressure of it all. As Alice Liddell, I could do and say whatever I liked, not many cared for the thoughts of a mad woman, but soon I would no longer be her. Or I mean, me. I'd be his wife, and that entailed so many more things than I knew what to do with.

"Have you caught your breath?" Rhoda asked, and I nodded. "Freddie, why don't you go on out? Give Alice a moment to collect herself. We'll follow shortly."

Fredrick's footstep moved away and then the door closed. Rhoda and I stayed by the window for a few moments longer, neither of us speaking. Then just when I was about to tell her I was ready, voices came near the window from below.

"I don't understand why you are marrying that mad girl." The voice belonged to Lewis's friend, Bart, a ghastly man who stared far too long at my little sister. "At least, marry the spinster. She seems to have a good head on her shoulders even if she's a bit older."

Rhoda and I exchanged a silent look, leaning close to the edge to hear my soon-to-be husband's response.

"Alice is perfectly handsome." At Lewis's words, Rhoda grinned at me. "Besides, I do not need a spinster with her nose in a book.

Maybe for after I've written mine, but that will never happen if I don't marry Alice." Lewis sounded exasperated as if he were tired of having to explain himself.

My brow furrowed in confusion. What book? I had never heard of Lewis writing a book.

"But why marry her? Don't you have enough material from her Wonderland nonsense? You could string her along for a few more months and then find someone more suitable."

I gasped, my hand going to my mouth. My eyes slowly turned to meet Rhoda. Her eyes reflected the horror in mine. Anger and confusion swirled inside of me, but I held them down until I could hear what else Lewis had to say.

"I am not a complete bastard." Well, that was soon to be determined. "I have strung her along for too many months as it is. People were starting to talk. If I don't marry her now, then she will have no hope for other prospects even if I cast her aside for someone else."

"Well, then." Bart slapped Lewis on the shoulder. "For your sake, I hope your new wife is a wanton thing and finds a lover quickly, then you can divorce her and be done with it."

The men continued to argue as they moved away from the house and toward the wedding party further inside the garden hedges. It was good and well because the fury inside of me, one I never knew I had, was ready to jump over the railing and pounce on their heads.

The audacity. The sheer abhorrence of that man. How dare he think that he could use me that way? My stories were not for his personal gain. They were mine and my father's. It was the one thing I had with him that no one else did. I could keep his attention with no end just by telling him of the wondrous things I saw while I dreamed. And for Lewis to take that... to corrupt it for his personal gain? I couldn't forgive him.

"Alice?" Rhoda placed a hand on my shoulder. "There are worse reasons for someone to marry. It doesn't have to be the end. Perhaps this will be the start of your own fantastical love story?" She smiled at me then, patting my shoulder. "Two unlikely people come together for their own reasons only to find love in the end. Doesn't that sound like the perfect sort of fairy tale?"

Yes, if that were the likely ending. I already knew how this story would end. Lewis would get his story, and I would be a divorcee. I'd never get a chance to marry again, and society would shun me. I could only pray we didn't have children before that point. I didn't worry about being caught cheating on my husband as Bart had hoped.

At this point, I never wanted to look at another man again.

Remembering my sister was waiting for an answer, I swallowed hard and nodded. "Of course. Can you give me a moment? I want to pray before the wedding."

"Certainly." Rhoda kissed my cheek before moving away. My eyes stayed on the garden outside, the wedding guests' voices drifting toward me in the air. The garden, once beautiful to my eyes, might as well have been dead and burned for all it stood for now.

"Alice?" Rhoda's voice said, quiet and unsure.

I turned my gaze away slightly. I thought she had left.

"You can make your own path. You are only trapped if you want to be." She cleared her throat and shifted uncomfortably. "I'll give you a moment."

My lips tipped down at my sister's advice, my eyes turning back to the gardens before me. I had no intention of praying. God shouldn't have anything to do with the fury in my heart. I stared hard at the green hedges, the rainbow of colors that should never be tainted by this day. With a sad sigh, I turned from the scene, but a movement in the corner of my eye caught my attention.

Spinning back around, my eyes narrowed, searching for the movement. There! A speck of white. A hint of a long ear. Now normally, I would just brush aside the sight of a rabbit in a garden. There really wasn't much remarkable about a rabbit.

However...

When the rabbit stopped at the edge of the hedges just a few feet from my window, giving me a clear view of him, I paused. My eyes widened, and I rubbed them, thinking I must have dozed off. But no, it was still there. The rabbit in a waistcoat. As if sensing me staring at it, he lifted up a pocket watch and tapped it, giving me a chastising wag of his finger, before darting off into the bushes.

What in the world?

Turning away from the window, I sped for the door. Not worried about being seen, I pulled open the door and headed down the stairs. My sister Rhoda stood in the salon, her eyes shooting to me as I made my way down the hallway and toward the back door.

"Alice?" she called out to me, but I ignored her, holding my long skirt in my hands as I picked up my pace.

I could still hear her voice still calling after me even as I pushed the back door open and stepped out into the garden. My eyes scanned the garden searching for the rabbit, but it was gone. I stomped my foot and growled.

"There you are." Rhoda breathed, grabbing my arm. "I was calling your name, didn't hear me?"

"Sorry." I only half turned toward her, my eyes still searching for the rabbit. "I thought I saw something."

"Oh, Alice." She breathed, brushed my hair away from my face. "Let's not start that again. Everyone is waiting for you." She looped her arm with mine and directed me toward the opening of the hedge garden where Fredrick waited.

"Alice, there you are." He took me from our sister and turned us toward the entrance of the wedding party. "I was beginning to think I'd be walking down the aisle alone. Wouldn't that be a sight?" he jested, trying to urge a smile from me.

I obliged, giving him a tight grin. "I'm here now."

"Well, then." Fredrick exchanged a worried look with Rhoda before inclining his head toward the garden. "You should take your seat. We'll be along shortly."

"Right." Rhoda hugged me slightly before disappearing into the garden.

My grip tightened on Fredrick's arm, and I licked my lips. Was I really going to go through with this? Could I? I'd never get another chance at marriage, but what Lewis had said still stabbed at my heart. It would be one thing to be marrying me for my money, which I had none, but Wonderland was precious. I couldn't just hand it over to him, could I?

"Alice? Alice." Fredrick squeezed my arm, jerking my eyes to his face. "It's time."

The wedding procession began, and our feet started to move. A part of me only half-realized what I was doing. The other half told me it was okay, that this was what was expected of me. I wouldn't be a burden anymore even if Lewis never learned to love me.

My feet hit the carpeted runner, and the eyes of our guests shifted toward me. I could feel them on me, boring into my clothing and skin, wiggling around like worms under my flesh. My fingernails bit into Fredrick's arm, but if it bothered him, he didn't show it.

We moved up the aisle one torturous step at a time. At the end of the path, Lewis stood with the magistrate. His hands were folded in front of him, his eyes focused on me. A small smile sat on his face as if he hadn't been talking about divorcing me not ten minutes ago. The reminder made the forced expression of joy on my face falter. I pushed it back up before anyone could notice.

When we came to the end of the line, something moved to the left of me. The rabbit again. My eyes jumped between it and the altar. Closer now, I could see the rabbit wasn't quite like any other I'd ever seen. His ears hung down to his feet, and the claws holding the pocket watch were long and sharp. The irritable expression on his face went along with the long, short-haired tail that tapped the ground, its fluffy end the only rabbit-like feature.

"Alice." Fredrick hissed in my ear, turning my attention from the rabbit back to the man I was about to marry.

Lewis stood there with his brows raised, a bemused expression on his face. He thought my behavior was funny, did he? Where his confusion might have made me laugh in other situations, this time it only fueled my anger. Well, let's see how amused he would be by this.

Jerking my arm free of Fredrick, I stumbled away from him. Passing my horrified mother and a smirking Violet, Rhoda was the only one who didn't seem surprised by my actions, but I only spared her a brief look before chasing after the white rabbit.

CHAPTER

THE GASPS OF HORROR followed me as I ducked into the hedge garden surrounding the wedding party. I could hear the shouts of my family calling me back, but I ignored them, my eyes set on the rabbit creature hopping at lightning speed just before me.

It dodged, I weaved. The chase carried on through an archway and into a part of the garden I'd never seen before. Here, the hedges were closer together, and a dark, ominous foreboding came over me as my feet kept pace with the rabbit. When the hedges gave way to a large tree in the center of a pretty courtyard, I slowed.

My head turned this way and that, taking in the surrounding area. This was new. I could have sworn I'd walked every inch of this garden, if not with Lewis than with one of my sisters. Scowling at my lack of memory of it, I glanced down at my dress. Dirt and sticks from my run had caught onto the lace fabric, tearing it in a few places.

"And Violet wanted me to wear white," I muttered to myself, pulling at the sticks and tossing them aside.

A thud followed by a breaking of branches drew my attention. My head jolted to the tree in front of me, my eyes widening as the rabbit creature crept closer to me. His nose twitched, and his beady black eyes gleamed, his tail moving back and forth like a clock pendulum.

"Hello there," I lowered my voice to a non-threatening whisper, holding my hand out to it to sniff. "What's your name?"

The rabbit cocked his head to the side, staring hard at my hand. "I'm not going to lick your hand, if that's what you're going for."

Startled, I pulled my hand back. "Oh, I'm sorry. I didn't realize you could speak." I sank to the ground, spreading my skirt out around me. "I'm Alice. Alice Liddell." I paused and then muttered. "Well, for now."

"I know who you are, why else would I have come?" The rabbit made an impatient sound, clacking his sharp fangs against one another. "I'm Watch, and you're late."

"Watch?" I peered down at him. "That's a curious name."

"Well, it's not my only name, but the only one you're getting." He turned and waved an arm over his shoulder. "Are you coming or not?"

Frowning at the talking rabbit, I hesitated. Was this a dream? Had I fallen asleep by the window, having gone into shock from Lewis's words? I glanced back from the way I had come, listening for anyone coming after me. When I heard nothing, I shrugged.

What did it matter? If it were a dream, I'd wake up by the end, and if anything, it'll give me time to figure out what to actually do about my situation. However, if it wasn't, then the problem was moot in any case.

"Alice," Watch snapped, already near the trunk of the tree, "time is almost up. You must decide."

Not waiting another moment, I climbed to my feet and hurried after him. "I'm coming."

Watch didn't wait for me before jumping into a hole at the base of the tree. A little, startled noise left me, and I rushed to where he had fallen. The hole was no bigger than my head, far too small for me to fit into or even that rabbit.

Leaning forward, I tried to peer into the hole without falling in, but the moment I came close to the opening, a sucking sensation overcame me. A scream ripped from my throat. My body squeezed and forced into the small hole, and I thought for a scary moment that I might be crushed to death. Then, before I knew it, I was thrown out the other side.

Breathing heavily, my heart pounding against my chest in rapid fire, I didn't bother trying to sit up from where I laid on the floor. The cold ground felt good pressed to my hot cheeks, despite the solid surface. A drowning quiet filled my ears, different from in the garden where there were the sounds of animals and people. Even a breeze made a sound, and it was that silence that alerted me to the conundrum I was in.

I lifted my head briefly. My eyes blinked open, wincing against the bright white before me. The floor was white. The ceiling and even the walls, if what I saw actually were walls, were all white, a startling white that burned the eyes.

"Are you going to lay there all day?" a squawking voice snapped at me from a little bit away.

"I figure she is because she's not moving. Perhaps she's dead?" another voice much like the other commented, though a bit too gleeful at the prospect of my demise.

"If so, we could eat her. We haven't had human in a while," the first voice announced, and with that, I was on my feet in a flash.

"I'm alive. No one is eating me." My words fell off my lips as my eyes found the ones who had spoken... or rather things. More talking animals. Now I was sure I was in one of my dreams.

A two-headed bird wearing an orange dress covered in embroidered flowers sat behind a wooden desk. A pair of spectacles sat on each of their faces, the faces that had beaks and feathers instead of hair. Beady eyes watched me with a sharp precision only a predator would use. At my words, they harrumphed and placed their feathered wings on their large hips.

"Well, if you would stop lying around like road kill then you wouldn't have an issue, now would you?" the left head said, waving her feathered wing at me.

"Roadkill?" I arched a brow at them.

Not answering my question, the right head shoved a board with a paper attached to it. "Sign in. Then some questions will be answered."

I picked up the board and stared down at the page. Columns for name, date, and realm were written across the top of the page. Beneath that was several scribbled names, one of which belonged to Watch. Where did that rabbit get off to?

But I didn't ask what I was thinking.

"Where am I?" My eyes moved from the page to the area around us, still an empty white nothing surrounded us. Only the circular desk with the two-headed bird woman broke up the endless white.

The two exchanged a look before the one on the left answered, "The Between."

"Between?" My brow rose exponentially. "Between what?"

The head on the right squawked loudly in what I thought to be a laugh. "Why, everything. Where else would you put a between?"

I pointed the pen around us. "What's on the other side of this between?" And how in the world did I get out of it? The last part I didn't ask. I was already pushing my luck as it was with the two before me... or would it be one?

"Well, that depends on where you want to go," the right head answered with a snap of her beak.

I didn't know where I wanted to go, only that I had been searching for something. What had I been searching for? Oh, yes.

"Have you seen a rabbit around here?" I asked, remembering my original course. "He said his name was Watch."

The head on the left scratched its chin and then turned to itself. "Type, did you see a rabbit?"

"No, Gripe. The only person who came through here was that Opalaught. What was his name?" Type asked her other head, searching around the area.

"An opalaught?" I raised a brow. "What's an opalaught?"

Ignoring me once more, Gripe answered, "That one's name was maybe something like Clock? Tick? Something to do with time, I'm sure."

Frustrated by their blatant disregard and overall silliness, I slammed the board on the counter. "Watch. The rabbit's, I mean, opalaught's name is Watch. Now, which way did he go?"

The two of them stopped jabbering to themselves and stared at me. After a long, tense moment, Gripe pointed a finger at a door behind her.

Hold on. A door? When did that show up?

I glanced around me and realized there were more doors. "Where did those come from?"

"They've always been here," Type snipped. "You just weren't looking."

Giving Type a glower, I moved away from the desk and toward the doors. One sat in the direction in which I had come from. I shook the handle and found it locked. Frowning, I moved around to the next door, the second of the four doors which had suddenly appeared in the middle of the white room, or rather abyss. I wasn't quite sure what else to call it. I couldn't see any corners or ways out beside the doors. I hesitated to move past them in fear I might become lost.

The second door's handle was also locked, as was the third and the fourth. Curiously, the latter, in addition to being locked, had chains wrapped around the door with more than a dozen locks on them.

"You won't get in there," Gripe called out, reminding me they were there.

"More importantly, you don't want to." Type nodded her head with a warning look in her eyes.

"Alright," I drew out coming back to the desk, "then how do I leave? Watch said I was late, but he didn't very well wait for me. How do I know where to go?"

"Well, let's see." Type picked up the board and read the contents through her spectacles. "Watch signed back in from the human realm several hours ago." She stopped and peered up at me. "You are quite late, aren't you?"

"Hours ago?" I cried, my mouth falling open. "But I just saw him not a few minutes before." I gestured back toward the door I'd come from.

Gripe shrugged. "Time flies here faster than you can blink, especially for a human. You'd think you'd remember that from before."

"Before." I mouthed. "Right. Well, in any case. I need to go where Watch went. Does it say where he went next?" I pushed up on my tiptoes and tried to see over the board, but Type pulled it tighter to her chest, sneering.

When I sighed and dropped back to my feet, she finally looked at the paper. "Ah, ha." She tapped a feathered wing on the paper. "He went to Summerville." I must have looked confused because she added on, "That's in the Seelie Court."

Seelie Court? Summerville? "Isn't this Wonderland?" I frowned their words foreign to me.

"Wonderland. Wonderland?" the two heads squawked together and chatted as if I wasn't even there.

"She thinks we're in Wonderland."

"What the hell is Wonderland? Been drinking too much tea, that one." Type nodded in agreement with her other head.

"Humans are quite mad. Didn't you know? Better to send her off to the queen."

"No, no. The opalaught will be needing the credit. Better send her to him," Type told Gripe with an annoyed glance at me. "Better to put the blame on him for leading her here in the first place."

"Enough," I snapped, banging my hand on the counter. "This is my dream! I'll decide where I go."

An amused look passed between them, then Gripe gestured toward me. "By all means, Alice, where do you want to go?"

"The rabbit, I mean, the opalaught, Watch. Where did he go?" I placed my hands on my hips, staring the two of them down.

Their shoulders lifted in what I supposed was a shrug before Type answered, "We've told you. Summerville. Though you are quite a bit behind."

"Days," Gripe interjected.

Throwing up my hands and deciding to just go along with it, I asked, "Which door sends me there?"

"That one," Gripe pointed at the one behind them, "but you can't get in there. You need a key." She pulled a key on a long ribbon out of her dress. "Just like this."

I stared at the key for a moment, and then the door, and then locked eyes with the bird. "And how does one get a key?"

Snorting, Gripe swung the key back and forth as she taunted me with it. "You need permission."

Knowing where this was going, I decided to skip the questions and take matters into my own hands. "What's over there?" I pointed toward the big white area off in the distance.

Gripe and Type turned their heads toward where I pointed, and instantly, I took the chance to snatch the ribbon out of her hand. Before they could stop me, I gathered my skirts and raced around the desk to the door.

It took longer than I expected for the two of them to notice. The squawks of alarm only sounded once I had the key in the hole. I twisted the key and opened the door. Before I could step through, something caught my train, and my skirt ripped, plunging me head first through the doorway.

41

CHAPTER

I BRACED MYSELF FOR impact, but the world around me slowed, my descent with it. The Between had disappeared, and I was falling through what looked like a rabbit hole.

Covered in dirt, the walls moved at a languid pace or rather I did. My torn skirt flared out around me like an umbrella, and I scrambled to make sure I wasn't showing anything important. When I failed to make my skirt stay down, I sighed.

Well, it was a dream after all. No one back home would know they had seen my undergarments. My train had already been destroyed which took the majority of the back of my dress with it. I should be happy to have any dress left at all. Now if only my corset would meet the same gruesome fate.

The door I'd fallen through must have been far above me, but I couldn't see it beyond the darkness. The ground was far beneath me. So far that I couldn't see what lay below.

Glancing up from the ground, there were cabinets filled with odd bottles and objects. Glass mirrors hung from odd angles. One showed me upside down. The other a gruesome decomposed form. I flinched away from the mirrors in time to see the walls around me fill with clocks.

All shapes and sizes ticked in my ears though when I peered at the time each of them said something different. Some were like normal clocks, but the time was all wrong, the hands spinning wildly in circles around the face. The others had odd letters I didn't understand or sometimes not even numbers or letters at all. I saw a picture of the sun, a snowflake, a red leaf, and a flower circled one face. Did they track the seasons like this? With the way Gripe and Type had spoken about me being behind, I couldn't imagine it to be easy. One moment was hours. A few minutes ended up being days. How did one know day from night in this place?

43

Thinking about time made me wonder about home. How long had I been gone? Had they stopped searching for me? Or had my family found me, and at this moment, I was lying in bed dreaming this dream?

"More like a nightmare," a teasing voice growled at me from below.

My eyes shot down, searching for the owner of the voice as my descent came to a sudden yet not at all painful stop. My heels clicked against the red tiled flooring as my feet touched down, and I turned in a circle in a shock to take in this new place.

A mixture of mismatched furniture lay spread out around the medium size room. Clocks were the primary decoration here as well, though one large grandfather clock dominated one of the walls, its pendulum swinging back and forth in a hypnotizing manner. Shaking my head, I backed away from it and searched once more for the voice. I knew I hadn't imagined it. Why would I? I was dreaming after all, a dream that I was starting to wish I'd wake up from soon.

"Why, that's no fun at all." The voice graced me with its presence once more. My head swiveled toward the sound, landing on a tall-backed armchair with an orange ball of fur sitting in it.

Moving closer, I spoke this time out loud, the thought of whoever or whatever this was reading my mind too strange for even me. "Hello? I apologize for dropping in like this. I was on my way to Summerville." I paused, waiting for an answer. When none came, I continued, "I came with Watch?"

A low growl came from the orange fluff, and a tail unwrapped from around itself. That single tail became larger and multiplied until there were nine tails in all surrounding the frowning face of a fox. Could foxes frown? A question for another day.

"Watch. Watch. Everyone cares about that damn opalaught." The fox snapped his jaws, and I flinched back. "Like he could be trusted to keep the time. He's always late."

My head cocked to the side, peering over the talking animal. He wore a buttoned-up sapphire vest with gold clocks decorating the fabric. The buttons were also clocks. It seemed the obsession with time didn't just stop at the decor.

Clearing my throat, I knelt down to the fox, so I was at eye level with the three-foot fox. "Hello, my name is Alice. Could you help me?"

The fox stopped preening and complaining long enough to focus those beady black eyes on me. Licking his jaw, a slow, wicked grin curled up his face. Still astounded by the fact that the fox could actually make a facial expression, I almost missed what he said next.

"I could, but I won't."

I frowned. "Why not?"

"Because I'm bored, and you are quite the interesting piece of something else." He licked his paw, his eyes glinting at me in such an obscene manner that I feared he might want to eat me. He climbed off the chair and stood before me, taking my hand in his paw. I forced myself to stay still in case he might bite.

"Tell me, Alice." He snapped his jaw as he hissed out my name. "How do you feel about becoming my companion and, perhaps one day, my wife?"

My mouth gaped. "Why... uh... I'm flattered, but I don't even know your name and, where I'm from, marrying an animal is unheard of, talking or otherwise. So, I'll have to decline politely." I withdrew my hand from his paw and took a step back with what I hoped was a disappointed look.

Unfortunately, my word did nothing to dissuade the fox, he looped his thumbs - were they thumbs? - into his vest and grinned up at me.

"My apologies. You may call me Tick, and as for my form..."

His tails wrapped around him, and he twisted in place before growing larger, transforming right before my eyes. The fur pushed back to reveal muscular olive skin, enough skin to make me blush. The vest strained against the bare chest beneath, and his hind legs were now long and lean, covered in pants made of what seemed to be leather.

After getting over the initial shock of the transformation and - who was I kidding? - the lack of clothes covering parts I hadn't even seen on my brother since we were children, my eyes moved up to the strong jaw and sharp-angled nose. The orange fur that had covered his body now confined itself to a long mane hanging down his back and over his shoulder, silky and soft. My hands itched to touch it.

However, the beady black eyes which had changed into an ember hue warned me off. The glint of them that I could no longer mistake for that of a hungry fox was now that of a man looking at a woman and thinking of all the ways he could violate her.

"Is this form more to your liking?" A roguish grin curled his lips, a sharp canine peeking out. "Now, it does take a bit more energy than I usually like to expend on a daily basis, but for you?" He picked up some of my hair which had fallen out of the pins Violet had painstakingly put up and let it slide between his fingers before curling it tight and giving me a bit of a jerk. I either had to move toward him or risk my hair being yanked out.

I chose the former.

My choice placed me closer than I'd ever been to a man, even Lewis. We'd always had a chaperone, and even then, we always at least two feet apart. I certainly had never felt his breath on my face or the heat of his body so close to mine. The scent of Tick a spicy sort of flavor that caused a warmth to spread through my abdomen and brought on an involuntary press of my thighs. I had to admit, it wasn't a completely unpleasant feeling.

Clipping my mouth shut, I realized Tick was actually waiting for an answer. "Well, I wish I could but..." I withdrew from him, waving a hand at my destroyed dress and hair. "I'm actually getting married. I mean, I was until I saw that..." I trailed off my eyes leaving him and searching for a way out, not seeing anything but the large grandfather clock ticking aggravatingly in the background. "I really should find Watch and get back."

Tick's grin never faltered. "You don't sound so sure. Perhaps I could persuade you to stay." He waved an arm at a table with a teapot and a set of cups. My eyes darted from side to side, but I couldn't find a reason to tell him no, especially if I needed him to let me out of here.

Letting out a sigh, I took one of the seats and grimaced, shifting my dress so that the corset wasn't stabbing me. "So, since we are being civilized, could you answer a few questions for me?"

Tick took the seat across from me and crossed one leg over the other. His feet were bare which should have disturbed me but actually seemed normal. Why shouldn't he be barefoot? He was a fox. Fox didn't wear shoes. They didn't wear vests either, but here we were.

Pouring the tea, Tick eyed me over his cup. "How about we play a game instead?"

I arched a brow at him, picking my cup up but not drinking from it. "A game?"

"Yes." His tongue snuck out to catch the liquid on his lips, and my eyes tracked the movement. "I'll answer your questions, but you have to answer my riddle."

49

"Riddle?" I frowned. "I've never been very good at riddles." I lifted the cup to my lips but didn't a drink. "My sister Rhoda, now she has never found a riddle she couldn't solve. Violet, on the other hand, is a riddle in herself. One day, she only cared about bright colored clothing, the next, it was beige lace. Who knows what's actually going on in her head?" I sat my cup down and picked up the spoon, swirling it around in the liquid. Tick's eyes followed my every moment.

"Interesting. And your husband to be? What's he like?" Tick's tails appeared out of nowhere, making me blink rapidly. They swayed from side to side in a kind of lullaby that made my head feel heavy.

"Lewis? Well, he's..." I trailed off, having a challenging time getting my thoughts together. "He's all right."

"Only all right? I'd think you'd want more than just all right if you were marrying him. All right is for a meal with a long-distance friend, or perhaps a song, but never for a life partner. I could be so much better than all right... for you." He leaned forward on his elbows, my gaze drifted up to his eyes, my mouth drooping open.

"Huh?"

"We were discussing the game," he said smoothly. "I will ask you a riddle, and if you answer correctly, then I will show you how to find that damnable Watch. But if you lose..." He tapped his long nails on the table between us, arching over the space to press his face close to mine. That delicious smell of his invaded my senses once more, and I found myself moving closer to him.

"If I lose...?" I mimicked him, not really caring what he was talking about as long as he came closer.

"If you lose, then you have to marry me instead. Stay here forever." A wicked grin spread across his lips, his hand tipping up my chin to meet his gaze. "Do we have an agreement?"

"A what?" I blinked, my head not quite on right.

"Do you agree? To the rules of the game?"

"Oh, yes. Of course. The rules. We must follow the rules," I mumbled.

Tick seemed satisfied by the response and took his seat once more, leaving me hanging above the table on my own. Flopping back into my chair with a less than dignified huff, I lifted my cup to my mouth.

"Now, I only find it fair to answer your questions first so go ahead ask away." Tick waved a languid hand my way.

Questions? I had questions? If I did, I couldn't remember any of them now. I could hardly remember what I had been doing here in the first place. Tick had said something about a watch, but he had so many clocks already. Why would he need a watch? My eyes drifted to the grandfather clock again, then they followed the pendulum until I noticed a dark inkiness behind it. It wasn't the dirt wall, and a flicker of light moved in the blackness that had me sitting up straighter.

"What's behind that clock?"

Tick's brows rose high on his face, a look of astonishment replacing his bored amusement. "Behind the grandfather lies the lair of the JubJub and also so happens to lead to the streets of Summerville."

Summerville. Summerville. Why did that name sound familiar? Did I live there?

"Though I'm not sure why in the Underground you would want to go there. Nothing but stuck up Seelie piss ants. Your opalaught friend would be lucky to keep his head going in there by himself." Tick clucked his tongue and sipped his tea. "Now, if that was all your questions, my turn."

"Opalaught," I said, the feeling of the word strange inside my mouth but familiar as well. Summerville. Opalaught. It was on the tip of my tongue. I'd been trying to find an opalaught in Summerville. Why? Why? Why?

52

The fox in human form kicked my chair with his bare foot, jolting me from my thoughts. "Are you ready for my riddle, Alice? Or would you prefer to watch me for a little while longer? I'm happy either way."

Watch! My eyes widened as I realized what I'd forgotten. I'd followed a rabbit wearing a waistcoat down a hole. The rabbit's, opalaught's, name was Watch, and this sly fox before me was trying to drug me into compliance with both his presence and with the way he was urging me to drink, most likely his tea.

I snapped my mouth shut and shook my head, clearing the last of the fog away. Sitting my undrunk cup on the table before me, I pushed my seat back. "You, sir, do not fight fair. I will not be bamboozled by a cheat and a liar."

"But rules are rules, dear Alice." Tick lounged back in his chair, twisting his finger in a circular motion above his cup and causing the contents inside to spin on its own. "You have already agreed. The game has begun. No backing out now."

I placed my hands on my hips and glared. "An agreement made under false pretenses such as drugging your visitor. What kind of person," I caught myself and flung an arm at him, "thing are you?"

Tick stood from his seat, a smirk on his lips. "Why, I'm Fae, I would think you would remember? Though, you are a bit older than the last time you stopped by." His eyes scanned up and down my form. "Not that I'm complaining. However, if you don't remember you being here, then there's no hope for you to stay. You had promised to play my game when you were older, but it seems like you aren't quite old enough." He picked up my hair and gave it a sniff, making a face. "Yes, yes. I was right before. Not old enough for me. Now off you go. You're terribly late, you know."

I gasped and jerked my hair from his hands. "I cannot decide if I should be offended or pleased. I do know that I am annoyed and quite through with this silliness. And of course, I've been here before. It's my dream... but why in the world I would dream up someone like you, I will never know." I huffed and turned on my heel marching to the clock. "Good day."

"Good night." The fox waved his fingers at me before transforming back into his original form and curling up on the chair. Before placing his head down, he angled it toward me. "And do be careful of the JubJub. She can be quite the little bitch when woken up."

Ignoring his foul language, I pulled open the door to the grandfather clock and, careful of the pendulum, walked inside only to be surrounded by complete darkness.

CHAPTER 5

WHEN MY FOOT HIT solid ground, I let out a relieved breath. I wasn't sure my heart could take anymore falls, or my dress. Well, what was left of it.

Sadly, having a place to stand on was about the only good thing going for the JubJub lair. I'd never been to a lair, let alone even knew what one was. If I had to imagine a lair, there would be quite a bit more light and a lot less of a dead rat smell.

I inched further into the blackness, my hands reached out in front of me to search for anything I might run into. They first found the dirt wall next to me. I kept one hand on the wall to my right and followed it as I moved through the dark. The light I had barely caught sight of before was nowhere to be seen.

It came to my attention that I should have been terrified. This whole scenario was something straight out of a nightmare, walking in the dark in a strange world, not the Wonderland I remembered certainly. I remembered talking animals, musical tea parties, and mad queens, not sly foxes with a scent that still made me weak in the knees or dark lairs that had a hint of copper in the air.

The darkness was disconcerting. If it were really my dream, I could make a light, couldn't I? I closed my eyes for a moment and concentrated on making a light. Either my prayers had been answered, or I'd died, because there was finally a break in the black abyss.

Blinking against the light, I started toward it. The surrounding walls tightened, and I no longer needed to keep my hand on it to find my way. Soon, I was crouching down to my hands and knees. If I wasn't already wearing a corset, I would need one to suck in enough to get through the hole the pathway had turned into.

When the walls expanded again, giving me enough room to breathe, I moved to stand up. A low growl made me freeze. Stock still on my hands and knees, my hose ripped up from scuffing the floor and arms were

57

covered in scrapes, I strained my ears. When silence met me, I began to move again. This time, the growl turned into a mighty squawk that shook the walls around me.

The light I had been following darted to the right around a large form. It snapped its beak at it, blood shot eyes barely visible in the light as it rushed to get away from the beast.

The JubJub.

My heart pounded in my chest at the sharp beak snapping at the light which was growing dimmer by the moment. It was only a dream, Alice. Remember, it can't hurt you.

Still, I didn't want to be in the dark alone with that monster. I climbed to my feet and raced after the light. I dodged left as a large bony wing slammed down where I had been standing before letting out a small squeal of fright. That one sound drew the JubJub's attention away from the light to me. Its bony wing pounded the dirt as it shifted around to get to me.

I didn't give the thing the chance.

Throwing myself in an opening between the JubJub's wing and body, I barely escaped its snapping beak as I rolled onto the ground and back up to my feet. Not waiting to see if it followed me, I ran in the direction the light went. I could still see it, just a tiny ball in the distance and hurried to catch up to it, the JubJub squawking behind me.

My foot caught on what was left of the front of my dress and I tripped, falling face forward on the ground. My chin burned where it scraped the dirt. The JubJub was closer now, not giving me a chance to recover from my fall. I crawled to my feet, gathering my skirts into my arms.

Someone seeing my drawers was the least of my worries right now.

Lungs burning, I thought the tunnel would never end. The JubJub certainly wasn't getting tired, but I had to keep moving. Even if this was a dream, I didn't particular care to know what it feels like to be eaten alive.

Closing in on the light that had been leading me through the tunnel, it merged into a larger light. No, not a light. An opening. The exit!

The JubJub let out an annoyed squawk at the appearance of the exit and seemed to turn around, pounding the opposite way. Did it not like the light? Not waiting to see if it changed its mind, I rushed toward the opening.

Finally, I crawled out of the JubJub's lair, the sound of its cries echoing behind me. I glanced back at the dark nothing I had come from and wondered how exactly the buildings surrounding it didn't disappear into the darkness as well. It didn't make much sense, but then again, this was a dream. Nothing had to make sense.

I backed away from the entrance of the JubJub lair and walked toward the sound of life. People. The brick walls of the buildings around me were rough against my fingertips as I trailed them against the surface. Finally, something I recognized. There was even a road beneath my feet. However, that was where the familiarities ended.

Tall men and women with pointed ears and hair every color of the rainbow walked the streets. Some of their hair even matched their skin. I tried not to gape and stare at one of the purple-skinned beauties. I would have been fine if the only things wrong were their skin and hair, but the clothing! They were showing more skin than I did when I came out of my mother's womb.

I turned to stare at a beautiful woman. Taller than even my brother Fredrick who stood at six foot, her long black hair shined with blue streaks, her skin just as dark and covered in a gauze-like material over her breasts and nether regions. She might as well have been naked for all the good her clothing was doing. I couldn't understand why no one stopped and stared at her. It seemed as if no one saw anything out of the ordinary, not that they should.

Glancing down at my ruined dress, the light blue material had been stained into a muddy gray. My mother would die of humiliation if she had the chance to see me now, even more so if she had a chance to see the gorgeous man with tan skin and a golden mane of hair cut to the scalp on one side. The golden-brown loin cloth clung to his manhood but left his butt bare.

Dear Lord Almighty, was he lovely.

A couple of large men dressed in shining golden armor patrolled the streets with gleaming swords at their waist. They passed by my alley way, and I jerked back into the shadows. They stood out like a sore thumb among the other tall, beautiful people, and the others moved out of their way as they came by, caution and worry on their faces. I didn't need to be my sister Rhoda to know that it would not be a good idea to be caught by them.

I waited a few moments until the guards were gone and then took a tentative step out of the alley. A few eyes moved my way, lips curled in disgust at my attire, and one sniffed the air as if they could smell me from where they stood.

Well, they could just get over themselves. Did they think I wasn't used to being stared at? I'd been at the wrong end of the gossip line more than a few times over the years. Lifting my chin, I kept my eyes forward and pretended to know exactly where I was going.

Out of the corner of my eye, I caught sight of several shops. A pastry shop displayed tarts shaped like hearts in the window. I stopped before a window where Fae, at least that's what I assumed these strange folks were based on Tick's words, were eating oysters on wooden tables and, when they paid their bill, took the table with them. I backed up to read the sign. The Walrus & the Carpenter. Guess you could go into business with a worse person.

My stomach grumbled at that moment. and I contemplated seeing if they would feed me. After one more look at my clothes, I figured I probably should find something else to wear instead. Not that I had any money to pay with.

Before I could chance it, a hand clamped down on my arm. I let out a small squeak and pulled away, thinking the guards had found me. A hand wrapped around my mouth, cutting off my cries of alarm, and then next thing I knew, I was being pulled into a nearby shop.

The door shut behind us as I bit down on the hand over my mouth and jerked my arm hard enough that I felt something on the inside strain to the point of pain. Through my large skirt, I tried to kick at my assailant but couldn't get much of hit in through all the fabric.

"Calm down, human," a masculine voice with a rolling timber demanded.

I spun around, pulling my skirt up in preparation to kick the male in his most sensitive parts. A handsome dark-haired man with piercing green eyes backed away from me with his hands up. Tall and muscular, his sleeveless shirt stretched across his chest and a band with numbers and dashes wrapped around his arm. Deep brown pants covered his legs and calf-high boots tapped on the floor, clearly waiting for me to stop gawking at him.

"Who are you?" I placed my hands on my hips and hoped to sound commanding. "You cannot just abduct someone off the streets."

"I'd hardly call it an abduction." The man rolled his eyes and moved further into the shop. "More like a rescue from yourself. You were seconds away from being caught by the royal guard."

"That still does not give you the right to manhandle me in such a manner, sir." I waved a finger at him, my eyes taking in the surrounding room.

The shop I'd been dragged into belonged to a seamstress. A dais in front of several mirrors stood to one side along with several clothing racks. My abductor walked to a door in the back of the store and yelled, "Carban, she's here."

"You planned this?" I followed after him, my brow furrowed in confusion. "How did you even know I was coming?"

The person named Carban came barreling out of the back before the other one could answer. Glancing between the two of them, I realized they were twins. Not just any twins but the mouthwatering, please rescue me from myself kind of twins. The only difference between them was that Carban wore a jacket over his shirt, but he was no less attractive or in shape as his brother.

When the new set of green eyes settled on me, I clipped my mouth shut and forced my eyes to meet theirs.

"This is her?" Carban frowned and then looked at his twin. "Are you sure, Coby?" He glanced up and down my form, clearly finding me lacking.

"Of course, I am," Coby argued, waving a hand at me. "It's not hard to pick her out of a crowd. Blonde hair, blue eyes, a general lack of knowing what the hell is going on."

"I beg your pardon," I interjected.

Coby pushed past me and stopped at the counter where he began unwinding some lace. Only half paying me any mind, he picked up a blue corset and examined its ties. "You're the Alice, correct?"

It took me a moment to realize he was directing the question to me. "Yes, I'm Alice, but how did you know that?"

"Easy," Carban said as he moved to his brother's side and began looping lace through the corset. "The seer, Manciple, told us," he said as if I should know who he was talking about.

"No, not Manciple. It's Francis now, remember?" Coby reminded his brother, bumping him with his elbow. "And don't be saying their names." He clucked his tongue and picked up a pair of scissors to cut into some pale blue fabric on the table, except instead of cutting, the scissors fused the fabric to the other cloth beside it.

I found myself moving closer to them, intrigued by their work. They worked in sync as if they knew what the other person needed without having to say it. Their mouths were talking about something else entirely.

"Do not gripe at me about saying their names when you just did," Carban began.

"I did not," Coby snipped, holding the dress he'd been making up to examine it before continuing to use the scissors on it. "And you know how fucking stupid I find this whole no name bit."

"Excuse me." I huffed, crossing my arms over my chest. "I'm a lady. You shouldn't say such words in front of me."

"Which words?" Carban asked, a coy grin on his face as he paused in his lacing. "There were plenty of words just said. You have to be more specific."

A snort came from Coby. "Oh, Carban, she means the fucking word."

Carban arched a brow at me, coming around the table to face me. "Is it the word fucking itself or the act of fucking?" He tipped my chin up, his eyes darkening as he spoke. "Because anyone who doesn't like fucking hasn't ever been fucked by us."

I gaped, my breath caught in my chest. I couldn't decide if I was offended or aroused by their words. No one has ever spoken to me that way before. Certainly not Lewis.

"Come on now, take your dress off. We haven't got all day." Carban gestured a hand toward me as he removed his jacket, revealing a sleeveless shirt that matched his brothers.

My eyes grew to saucer size at his command. "I'm not having sex with you." My words came out a stutter and were only weakly filled with protest. I hated to admit how much the idea of these two gorgeous men fucking me actually appealed to me. Far more scandalous than anything I'd have ever dreamed up.

Carban and Coby exchanged a look, and then Coby replied, "That wasn't what we had in mind at all."

"We need to fit you for your dress," Carban licked his lips, his eyes trailing up and down, my form heating every inch of me with his gaze, "but we could always fuck afterward."

Coby whipped the dress they had been working on off the counter and grinned. "Quite, quite. That's if the dressing is right."

CHAPTER 6

I CLOSED THE BATHROOM door with a snap, my arms full of the dress the twins had made for me. How they even knew I'd been coming was still a bit fuzzy to me, but since it was a dream, I hardly thought it implausible. It certainly made the fact that the dress was exactly the size I needed all the more palatable.

Dropping the dress onto the top of the sink counter, I took a moment to appraise their plumbing. It was far superior to many of the ones in the homes I'd been too. It even beat Lewis's bathroom which was fitted with the most up-to-date toilets around. I wondered if they had hot water in their baths, as well, or one of those fancy showers?

A knock on the door followed by Carban's voice jerked me out of my thoughts. "Do you need a hand? I have two that are more than willing to help."

"No, I'm fine," I called back, staring hard at the door. I half thought he might ignore my words and come barging in anyway, but when the handle didn't turn, I sagged.

Once I was sure no one would be coming to 'give me a hand,' I reached to the back of my dress and came to my first obstacle. The buttons. If this had been any of my regular dresses, I would have easily been able to take it off within moments. However, wedding dresses weren't meant to be put on or taken off by yourself. After a few moments struggling to get the buttons undone, I collapsed in defeat.

Sitting on the floor, I contemplated the likelihood the twins would help me without taking advantage. I didn't want to keep wearing what had become of my wedding dress, but did that outweigh the possibilities of being at their mercy?

For a moment, my mind wandered to what it would be like to be kissed by either of the twins. My face heated, and I smiled to myself at the thought. My skin prickled with anticipation of how they would feel pressed against me, their muscles bunching beneath my hands. An aching sensation starting from the inside and settling in between my thighs confused me.

I might be innocent in many ways, but I still knew what happened between a man and a woman. I also knew despite my mother's words of "Lie back and think of England," the mentality that relations between a man and woman could be quite enjoyable. Otherwise, my sister Rhoda wouldn't sneak out to spend so much time with the butcher's older son.

She'd leave in the dead of night and come back with her hair mussed and her cheeks flushed. I convinced her to tell me about her escapades with her lover, and while she kept the details pretty vague, I still was able to conclude that sexual relations might not be as horrible as my mother made them out to be.

Since I couldn't get my clothes off, I worked on my shoes and stockings. My shoes weren't practical by any means, but they were better than nothing. I sat the short-heeled shoes to the side and dragged my stockings down my legs, wincing as the material caught on the wound.

"Well, those don't look good at all."

My head jerked up to see Carban and Coby standing in the doorway. When had they opened the door? Ignoring his words, I hurried to cover my legs back up and forced a glare on my face.

"Do you mind?"

Coby smirked and knelt beside me. "Not at all. Carban, get the healing paste out of the cabinet up there." He pointed behind me where my clothing sat on the counter.

Carban moved to do so, but I didn't take my eyes off Coby who had taken hold of the bottom of my skirt. His eyes met mine, asking for silent permission, and I gave a cautious nod. My heart pounded in my chest, growing faster for each inch of flesh that appeared for their electric gaze.

Tutting as he shook his head, Coby drew my skirt up to mid-thigh and folded it over before going any further. The leg of my drawers was pushed up with it to reveal the extent of my injuries. The cuts were much worse than I had initially thought, and the longer I looked at them, the more they hurt.

"If I'm dreaming, I shouldn't feel pain, right?" I wondered out loud.

That gained a curious look from the twins. "Dreaming or not, these need to be cleaned or risk infection." Coby took the jar filled with a shiny white substance from Carban. Opening the top, a nice floral scent filled the air. "We can't have you dying on us before you can do what you came to do."

I frowned. "And what's that?" I blew a harsh breath between my teeth as Coby balmed my wounds. The cream might have smelled pleasant enough, but it stung worse than my monthlies.

"What's what?" Carban knelt behind me and worked on the buttons on my dress. I glanced over my shoulder at him, but he simply undid the buttons and started on my laces, not once straying to touch my skin. A small pang of disappointment went through me.

"What am I supposed to do?" I asked softly.

"About what?" Coby asked as he wrapped my leg with a piece of cloth. Each brush of his fingers against my thighs caused my throat to hitch and my breath to come out quickly. Coby's eyes met mine and an arch of his brow told me he knew exactly how he was affecting me.

I forced myself to breathe like a regular person and not some crazed harlot, then gave an aggravated shake of my head. I shifted out from under his hands and stood, my hands going to the front of my dress to keep it from falling. "It is impossible to ask you two anything."

72

"Not if you ask the right questions," Carban murmured by my ear, sending a shiver through me.

I spun around and pointed a finger at him. "Keep your distance, good sir. While I appreciate your help with the guards, I do not know you or your intentions. I'd like to keep my honor while I can."

The twins chuckled darkly before Coby took a step forward and bowed elaborately. "My apologies, Alice. I am Coby of the Needle clan, and this is my brother Carban."

"We have been tasked by the seer to guide you on your journey." Carban picked up the dress behind me and held it out above me. "Lift your arms."

I glanced at the two of them, pursing my lips tight. "Close your eyes."

Sighing as if it were all a big bother, Coby covered his eyes with his hand.

Then Carban closed his tight and said, "Come now, we haven't got long before the guards sniff you out."

"Sniff me out?" I asked, dropping my dress and corset and leaving me in my chemise and drawers. At least they weren't too dirty. My drawers had seen better days. I tried to put my arms in the dress, but Carban shifted it away from me.

"Those too." He pointed a finger at my undergarments, his eyes still closed tight. "As far as your question, you're human. You have a particular scent to you." He and his brother took a deep inhale of breath, a rumbling groan leaving their throats and making me blush. "Hard not to notice. Now, take the rest off."

My lips twisted in a frown, staring up at him as if he had to be peeking. "I won't be properly dressed."

Coby lifted a shoulder, and a slow smirk slid up his lips. "Who is to say what is proper? You are in the Underground now. Proper is relative."

I shifted in place for a moment, fighting against twenty years of conditioning telling me I couldn't do as they asked. Then I remembered. It's a dream, and even if it wasn't, my mother wasn't there to chastise me for not being properly dressed. No one would know as long as I kept my skirts down. With the way my adventure had been going so far, that wouldn't be very likely.

"I need drawers at the very least," I argued, not completely convinced. "I'm not going to walk around with all my private parts free for anyone to grab at."

Coby snorted. "Nothing here is free, least of all your lady parts."

"Here, here," Carban added then gestured with my dress. "Let's get this on first then. We can worry about your... others." He said the words like it was something obscene as if he were thinking too deeply on what my others looked like. It made me shift and blush. Thankfully, they still had their eyes closed.

Sighing in defeat, I threw my chemise off and dropped my shorts. Coby made a sound that made me think he might be looking, but one sharp look from me and his eyes were screwed tightly shut. I lifted my arms and stepped toward Carban, allowing him to bring the dress down onto my shoulders.

The thin blue material was cool against my skin, making my nipple pebble and my skin tingle. The sleeves ended at my shoulders in bunched-up puffs of fabric. The bodice hung loose around my chest, each movement making the material skim across my chest in a teasing manner. The skirt hung down to my knees and flared out as I twisted from side to side. I definitely needed undergarments.

"Much better." Carban nodded and reached out to adjust part of the neckline. "I think we over exaggerated the bust line though."

Coby moved around us and picked up the matching corset. "That'll be fixed once we get this part on." He started to wrap the darker blue garment around my front.

My brows furrowed. "Why are you putting it on this way? The corset should go on the inside."

Coby snorted, lacing up the back. "What good is it then? If you get attacked, your dress will be destroyed."

Knocking on the front of the corset bones, Carban sniffed. "Nothing is getting through this baby. Made of goblin skin, the toughest around." I grimaced at the thought of wearing a goblin's flesh on my body, but then Carban let his fingers trail along the bones of the corset and the thoughts of flayed goblins left my mind. "We harvested the bones from the orc ourselves."

"An orc?" I gasped and grabbed my chest. The corset covered my breasts, cupping them and pushing them up to give my small chest the illusion of cleavage. "Does it have to be so tight?"

"You can't let the magic to escape," Coby explained, as if that were any explanation at all, tying off the bottom and then coming around. He tapped a finger against his bow-shaped lips, his dark brows bunched together in concentration. "I think we'll be alright, as long as she sticks to the back roads and stays away from any boggarts."

Carban snorted. "That's as likely to happen as we are to fight over a woman."

Coby grinned and then frowned at my hair. "Your hair has seen better days. Do you mind?" he asked before taking apart my mess of a hair do.

"What's a boggart and an orc?" I forced back a wince as Coby worked on my hair.

"An orc is a large monstrous motherfucker who would sooner chop your head off and eat it than ask your name," Carban explained, leaving the room briefly but still talking. I had to strain to hear him from the other room. "Their bones are great for armor and embedding magic into clothing, hence your corset." He came back into the room, holding out a silky piece of cloth with two leg holes, almost like a child would wear as a nappy.

I arched a brow, taking it from him. "What's this?"

Wagging his eyebrows at me, Carban gave me a wicked grin. "To guard your others."

I flushed and clutched the material to my chest, waiting for Coby to finish my hair.

Carban leaned against the sink and watched us with critical eyes. "As for boggarts, well, let's just hope you never have to meet one. They're worse than the orcs. At least you can kill an orc. Boggarts require special spells to get rid of them, and even then, it only works half the time. Those nasty buggers are worse than lice."

Coby pulled my hair this way and that and then, with a slight pinch, announced he was done. "Have a look."

I turned around to look in the mirror. To my surprise, my hair no longer resembled that a bird's nest. He had somehow, without any help from curlers or water, gotten my hair to fall around my face in soft curls, parts of it pinned up beneath a tiny top hat sat off to the side of my head. "Oh, my! Coby, you are a marvel. A real master with your hands."

Coby leaned against the counter on the other side of me, effectively placing me between both twins. He lifted one of the curls and tucked it behind my ear, his fingers brushing my cheek. "Oh, Alice. You have no idea."

Flushing, I ducked my head and moved out from between the two. "Uh, thank you. I'll remember that. So, orcs and boggarts. Are they Fae like you?"

Snorting, Carban ran a hand through his hair. "No nothing like us. While, they are Fae—"

"But Unseelie Fae!" Coby interjected.

Carban shot an incredulous look at Coby. "Yes, Lower Fae. We're High Fae."

"Alright, I have no idea what that means..." I trailed off and then a loud bang came from the front room. Coby and Carban darted for the door, waving a hand for me to hang back.

Coby started toward the front. "Why, hello, what can I do for you gentlemen this fine day?"

A clanking of metal echoed through the shop as an official voice demanded, "Where's the girl, Tweedle?"

"Tweedle. I see what you did there. Twins. Needle. Oh, how clever you are, my captain of the royal guard," Coby's voice rose in warning.

Carban ducked his head back into the room and gestured at my hands. "I'd put those on. The guards will not be gentlemen like as we."

I hurried to do as he said, not caring if he looked or not. "What's happening? Why do they want me?"

Carban pushed me further back into the bathroom and backed me up against the counter. I didn't have a chance to wonder why he was crowding me all of a sudden before his face was close to mine. "Humans are not allowed in the Seelie Court. The

79

Queen. She's crazy." He shook his head as the voice came closer. "There's no time for that. I apologize ahead of time for this."

Before I could ask what this was, his mouth was on mine. For a moment, I froze. Shocked that I was being kissed, my first kiss, and from a complete stranger in my dreams at that. Well, it could be worse.

When I didn't push him off, Carban's large hands cupped my face and angled it, his mouth capturing mine more fully. My fingers curled into the fabric of his vest as a small sound escaped from my throat. I couldn't be certain, but I think I liked kissing him. Or him kissing me. I wasn't doing much else but letting him have his way, something I planned to rectify.

I opened my mouth, my tongue tentatively dipping out to taste his lips. Carban groaned and ground his lower half against me, one hand leaving my face to drag my leg up over his hip. The hard feeling of his manhood against my core caused me to gasp, my head falling back. Carban didn't seem to mind, moving his lips to my bared neck.

Too consumed by the new sensations going through me at the hands of this stranger, I didn't realize we had an audience until Coby cleared his throat. "As you can see, captain. There's no human here. Only our lover, Ally."

Pushing at Carban to stop, I dropped my leg and adjusted my clothing. I didn't know what game they were playing, but if I wanted to stay alive, I would play along.

"Hello," I demurely greeted.

Carban moved to my side, wrapping an arm around my waist. "Captain, how are you? Did you need another adjustment to your armor? We'd be happy to take a look. No charge, of course."

The captain of the royal guards stared at us for a moment. He had large violet eyes and pale iridescent hair which peeked out beneath his golden helm. The clenching of his jaw and flaring of his nostrils told me he didn't believe our little ruse for a second.

"No, I do not need any adjustment. What I need is for you to come with me to the palace. The queen wishes an audience."

Carban stiffened beside me but had a broad smile on his face. "Of course, anything for the queen. We'll close up shop, escort Ally home, and then we will head to the nearest portal."

"No, now. Her too." The captain pointed at me. With that command, he gripped the hilt of his sword and whipped around, marching out of the bathroom.

CHAPTER

THE CAPTAIN AND HIS guards marched us out of the twins' shop and down the street. If I thought I was drawing attention before, now that I had the twins and guards with me, everyone was openly staring.

"Jeez, whisper for Reaper's sake," Coby groused, giving the onlookers a warning glare. "You'd think they'd never seen dead Fae walking."

"Dead Fae?" I gaped at him, fear clenching my heart.

Carban took my hand in his, squeezing it in reassurance. "Do not fret. We will do our best to keep you safe."

Coby snorted. "Do not make promises you can't keep. We'll be lucky to keep ourselves alive, let alone her."

"Enough of the chit chat." The captain shoved at Coby, making us all move faster. "You will be lucky to keep your heads. The queen is in a foul mood this day."

"When is she not?" Coby muttered, earning a chuckle from the other guards and a glare from the captain.

"What my brother means is… what could have irked our good queen so?" Carban asked as he tried to smooth things over, holding onto me even tighter as if someone might snatch me away at any moment.

"Her wedding gift—" one of the guards started to answer but was cut off by the captain.

"That is for the queen to answer. No more questions."

As we marched through the town, down a cobble street before all the other Fae, my mind began to whirl. From the kiss to the pain, I was beginning to think I wasn't dreaming anymore. If I wasn't dreaming, then that meant Wonderland was real, and I was living in it. To take that to its ultimate conclusion, that meant I had really run away from my own wedding - not really a terrible thing when I thought about it - and I wasn't asleep, so my family was probably fretting themselves sick wondering where I was.

Which also meant, I had actually kissed Carban.

"My first kiss," I breathed, earning me a curious look from Carban, but he didn't comment on it.

My fingers went to my still swollen lips and realized I wasn't upset about it. I supposed if I had to pick anyone to give my first kiss to, better a handsome magical creature than my lying fiancé... or would that mean he was my ex-fiancé now?

I shook my head. I'd figure out the semantics later. Now, I had to worry about keeping myself alive. I just hoped the queen they were bringing me to was not the queen from my dreams. That queen, from what I remembered, had been cruel and cold, cutting people's heads off left and right and completely obsessed with her flowers and what color they were.

I still didn't know what purpose I was here for. In my dreams, it had all just been having fun and getting away from my humdrum life. The way things were going now, well... sans the kiss... I wasn't having much fun.

Not to forget about this seer who claimed I was here for a reason. What reason though? What could I, a mere human, do in a world full of magical creatures who, I imagined, could kill me with a snap of their fingers?

My thoughts were put on hold as we approached a mirror on the edge of town. The mirror stood seven feet tall and had a silver ornate frame. It didn't have a holder to stand in or even a wall to lean it against. It just floated in the middle of the street.

I glanced at the others, but none of them seemed to think anything was out of place.

The captain barked at one of his soldiers who stepped forward and touched the side of the mirror. The surface rippled turning into a silver goo. Giving it a wary look, I dug my heels into the ground when the twins started toward it.

"Come on, it'll be fine, Ally," Carban murmured in my ear, brushing a hand along my back. "It's just a portal."

The first guard entered the goo. It enveloped first him, then the rest of the guards as they stepped forward, sucking them into the mirror's surface without a trace. Then Coby entered. When it was my turn, I swallowed hard, glancing around for any other way, but the longer I waited, the more the captain started to notice me.

"Is there a problem?" the captain asked, arching a pale brow.

I opened my mouth to answer, but Carban beat me to it.

"No, captain. No problem. Ally's just a bit nervous. She's never met the queen before." Carban tightened his grip on my waist, urging me to keep my mouth shut. "Let's go, Ally. The queen is waiting." He brought me up to the mirror and then, without warning, gave me a little shove.

Letting out a sharp cry, I fell into the mirror. The silver goo wrapped around me cold and weirdly tingly along my skin. Thankfully, the trip didn't take very long. I was in one second and out the next, falling into Coby's awaiting arms.

"Why, hello, what have we here?" Coby drew me to him, his hand low on my back, allowing me to get a big whiff of his delectable scent. I melted against him. The tips of his canines peeked out of his lips as he slid his tongue along his bottom lip.

I watched as his nostrils flared and his eyes widened. I thought he might kiss me like his brother did, but instead, he gave me a curious look before releasing me.

Carban followed through the mirror, identical to the one we had entered and stepped into the small receiving room where we now stood. The guards who had come before us waited by the door. They made no move to rush us, however. It seemed the queen wasn't in that much of a hurry.

"I didn't think you one to push your luck so soon, brother," Coby teased, making his brother flush with embarrassment.

"What did you expect me to do?" Carban muttered, crossing his arms over his chest. "They would have scented her a mile away. You're the one who said she was our lover."

Coby smirked and slapped him on the back. "I know, right? Quick thinking, huh? However, it seems like you're the one benefiting from my lie." His gleaming green eyes moved to me, clearly wishing he had been the one kissing me earlier. "I don't suppose you'd want to make it even and let me kiss you?"

I started to object and then glanced over at the guards who were watching us with growing interest. Lowering my voice, I snapped, "I don't think now is the time to be bartering for favors."

"So, that's a maybe?"

"Coby," Carban shook his head and walked toward the doorway, "let's go."

Letting out a disappointed sigh, Coby smiled and then offered me his arm. "My lady, let us go see what our fearsome Seelie Queen wants with us today."

I eyed him for a moment and then, seeing no threat of him trying to sneak a kiss in, I looped my arm through his and allowed him to lead me out the way Carban had disappeared through.

The receiving room morphed into a long hallway with a multitude of doors and mirrors lining the walls. There were a few Fae with a similar look to the twins, leading me to assume they were High Fae, then there were a few creatures I didn't recognize as any kind of animal I'd ever seen, but they all wore some kind of clothing. A vest here, a dress there. When I caught sight of a short, brown creature with a black beard and a red hat wearing only a shirt and no bottoms, I averted my eyes. It seemed the rhyme and reason to what they decided what was important to cover up seemed vastly different than home.

Coby let out a chuckle.

"What?" I jerked my eyes to his laughing face.

"If a pair of brownie balls are enough to embarrass you, you are going to be permanently red." His eyes rolled over to me with a charming wink. "Not that I'm complaining. I think red would look rather good on you. I just wonder how far down your blush goes." His eyes dipped down to my neckline.

I'd almost forgotten the dress I'd been put in had an almost obscene neckline. I was tempted to cover my chest but had a feeling that if I did, it would only encourage him more.

"I cannot help that you Fae are such wild creatures. At home, well, we have many rules on what one can and cannot wear in public," I explained to him, watching the walls as we moved past.

"And what happens if you broke those rules?"

I opened my mouth to answer and then snapped it shut, my brows drawing together. "Well, I'm not sure. I suppose your reputation could be ruined, depending on what you were wearing. Public nudity is certainly against the law. You could end up in jail."

"For showing what you were born with?" Coby gaped and then snorted. "It doesn't sound like a place I'd like to go. I need a bit of public nudity every once in a while. It keeps things lively."

I giggled.

"What? Do you think I'm kidding?" Coby arched a brow. "I'm a tailor. Believe me, I would love to not have to make clothing all day."

"Then why don't you do something else, if you don't like your job?"

Coby shrugged. "It's a family business, and there aren't many jobs for ones such as us. Not unless we wanted to royal consorts, and believe me, many might lead you to think they want to bed the queen, but no sane person would."

"Is she that hideous?"

Before Coby could answer, we turned and moved through an opening which led to a large open garden. Several dozen Fae in all manner of dress stood in a crowd around something going on further into the garden. I couldn't see Carban just yet and figured he was in the center with the main attraction, the queen no doubt.

Coby stopped us on the stairs leading into the garden. "Listen, all joking aside, the Queen might seem like a kind person, but it would be a lie. Do not let the smiling faces fool you. She's been known to get rid of those who cross her, and she won't think twice about killing a human. So, stay close to us, and don't tell her your name."

I tried to ask him what my name mattered, but he took my arm and dragged me into the garden. I searched for the red roses from my dream but didn't see any. My shoulders sagged. The queen couldn't really be that bad if she wasn't the mad Queen of

Hearts from my dreams. That woman was a nightmare.

We pushed through the crowd and entered the circular opening. In the center, my eyes immediately found Carban standing off to the side, a mallet in his hand and a pinched expression on his face. Near him stood a handsome man with blonde hair and pale blue eyes, clothed in a white suite. His presence and posture announced his importance, but the golden crown on his head claimed him as king.

The king seemed nice enough. He held a mallet as well and watched with adoration in his eyes as a beautiful woman in a white gown swung her mallet at a ball. The ball shot across the green grass and through a series of hoops. Unlike any game of croquet I'd seen before, the ball changed its path mid-shot and headed for another set of hoops. When it seemed like her ball would miss some of them, the hoops, which seemed to be made of plant roots, suddenly disappeared into the ground and shot back up in front of the ball until the ball finally bounced off a tall stick at the end of the field.

A round of applause followed by a small curtsy by the woman told me this was some good thing. This must be the queen. Her eyes shone with sparkles, a pale blue compared to the king's ocean colored eyes. Her white hair was braided and hung down her back, decorated by gemstones arranged in the shape of snowflakes. The golden crown on her head was much smaller than the king's, barely visible, but it wasn't like she needed it. Anyone could see that this graceful and stunning woman couldn't be anyone other than the queen.

"Come now, Tweedle," the queen's voice, a melodic sound, sang out, waving her mallet in Carban's direction. "It's your turn."

"As you will, Your Majesty." Carban gave a slight bow and then his eyes went down to the ball on the ground, a grimace his face.

I could see Carban's ball better than the queen's and realized with a gasp of horror that the ball wasn't just a ball at all. Inside of a clear sphere stood a wooden stick creature with large black eyes and bony wings. It screamed and cursed as Carban hit the ball, sending it across the field. This time, the ball did nothing to help Carban make his points. If anything, the little creature inside was trying to make him miss, as well as the root hoops which disappeared just as Carban was about to make them.

"That's too bad. Your turn, darling," the queen cooed at her king who took his turn. He didn't do as bad as Carban, but with a twist of his wrist, he made sure that he did make a few hoops, if not as many as the queen.

"Cheating bastards," Coby muttered beside me. "I don't even see the point of the game if you're going to make sure you win."

"Oh, but that's the point, dear Tweedle." The crowd went deadly still as the queen's gaze zeroed in on Coby and me. "I never play a game if I don't know I will already win. If I did, I wouldn't be queen."

"Of course, Your Majesty." Coby quickly dropped to one knee, bowing his head to the queen. "I meant no offense."

"Of course, you did." The queen let out a girlish laugh, making Coby tense on the ground. "But do not worry. I do not plan to take your heads today. I have a job for you two." She gestured her mallet at Carban and Coby but then stopped at me. Her elegant brows furrowed, and her lips pursed into a thin line. "I don't think I know you."

Coby pinched my ankle, and I bit the inside of my cheek to keep from crying out.

"I'm Ally, Your Majesty." When the queen kept staring at me as if she expected more, I added, "I'm an apprentice to the Tweedles. I'm going to be a seamstress."

"Oh, all right." The queen's gaze moved from me, seemingly bored with my presence already. She turned from us and lined up her shot once more, but this time, she kept speaking. "As you know the wedding is in a few days, I need you two to help with the preparations. Nothing can go wrong. Everything is riding on this wedding being a smashing success."

She hit her ball with a harder than needed whack which sent it spiraling into the air. Instead of going over the hedge wall, it stopped abruptly and flew back to the ground, finding its home through a series of hoops before once more hitting the stick.

Spinning around to face the twins, her icy blue eyes narrowed, "Do you understand what I'm telling you?"

"Of course, Your Majesty." Carban brought a fist to his chest and bowed slightly. "We will do our utmost to ensure the princess has no problems with her wardrobe."

"And anything else she might need," the queen snapped. "My cousin has decided to trim her garden recently, and my spies have yet to have a chance to regrow. You will be my new eyes and ears." She paused for a moment, waiting for the twins to consent. When they did so, she gestured her mallet toward me. "Take her with you. You never know when you need a slip of a girl to hide in the background."

My teeth ground together at her description of me. Why, I never! Slip of a girl, indeed. Despite my outrage, I knew better than to call her out. This was a queen, and if I wanted to keep my head firmly planted on my shoulders, I would keep my mouth shut.

The twins answered with a mutual, "Of course, Your Majesty," and then tried to usher us out of the garden, but the queen's voice stopped us.

"And Tweedles?" She gave us an icy grin. "If anything goes wrong, I will personally see to it that you never see this side of the Underground ever again."

CHAPTER

HAPPY TO BE OUT of the queen's eye but not sure where exactly we were going, I allowed the twins to escort me from the palace. I trailed after them as we walked through the courtyard. They had their heads close together and were whispering to each other.

"Pardon me," I pushed myself between them, my hands on my hips, "but could one of you tell me what is going on here?"

"We're going to a wedding," Coby said.

"It should be a great affair," Carban added, adjusting his vest.

Coby snorted. "That's if the groom behaves and the bride doesn't lose her head."

I pursed my lips, intrigued. "So, we're just going to help the bride get ready for her wedding? That's all?"

The twins exchanged a look and then Coby threw an arm around my shoulders. "You don't understand how important this wedding is to the Fae. The Seelie Princess and the Unseelie Prince are to be wed and join our two sides together forever."

"Harmoniously," Carban added.

"Erroneously," Coby countered. Carban was about to argue but then clipped his mouth shut with a nod.

"So, what are the issues?" I glanced between the two as we stopped before a door standing in the middle of the courtyard.

Coby smirked and looped his arms around my waist, drawing me close. "The issue, my dear, is that plenty of people would love our kingdoms to unite but there are—"

"—plenty who would want to see it fail," Carban cut him off.

"Yes," Coby growled, glaring at his brother for his interruption. "One of those people—"

"A thing, really. I wouldn't consider what's left of them to be a person." Carban picked at his teeth, but then stopped and arched a brow at Coby. "What?"

"Are you done? I'm trying to tell this story. You already got to kiss her. At least, allow me this one pleasure. Unless..." Coby grinned down at me. "Have you changed your mind and would like to make it even? Then we can both tell you the rest."

My hands sat on his chest, and I was tempted. Ooh, I was aching for it. If Coby kissed anyway like his brother, then I knew I would enjoy it. However, I'd been just shy of giving it all away in that bathroom, and now, knowing I wasn't dreaming, I wasn't sure my mother would quite approve.

"No, thank you. A kiss under duress is one thing. I do not think I'd be able to explain to my fiancé why I was kissing you as well." I pressed away from Coby, removing myself from temptation.

"Oh, but I thought you were dreaming? Isn't that what you said?" Coby flashed me a wicked grin. "Why tell your fiancé anything at all?"

I shook my head, smiling back despite myself. "If I was dreaming, I'd have woken up by now. There are too many factors stating that this is in fact really happening, and if that is so, I am deeply in trouble."

"Is that so?" Carban asked.

"Because," I scoffed, "I ran away from my fiancé mid-wedding. I don't know what it's like here, but that is a serious offense back home, one that my mother will never let me live down. To add to that, my fiancé would never take me back." Not that I wanted him back after what I heard.

"No, I've already ruined myself and will probably end up sent to some nunnery or worse the asylum." I sighed a bit dejectedly.

"Then all the more reason to just give in." Coby cupped my cheek and ran his tongue along his lower lip. "If all is already lost, then what's there left to lose?"

"Just tell me."

"What a pity." Coby pouted but then recovered in an instance. "Perhaps another time."

"Whatever makes you happy," I countered with a cheeky grin and then pushed by him to the door. "Where are we going?"

Carban moved to the door as well and placed a hand on the door knob. "To the Unseelie Court. That's where the wedding will be held, so that is where we must go."

"And we only have to go through here?" I pointed at the large white door, much like the one I'd come through the first time. It gave me pause. A nagging feeling made me stick my hand in the pocket of my dress and finger the key I had stolen from Gripe and Type. "Uh, this wouldn't happen to go to the Between, would it?"

Carban's brows shot up. "Why, yes. Have you been?"

"Of course, she's been." Coby smacked his brother on the back of the head, earning him a glower. "How else would she get here?"

Chewing on my bottom lip, I stepped away from the door. "Is there no other way to the Unseelie Court?"

The twins stopped arguing for a moment to look at me, and then Carban answered, "Yes, but it would take days rather than minutes to get there."

"It's more dangerous as well."

I avoided their curious gazes while I tried to think of an explanation. "I... I want to see Wonderland. I mean, the Underground. I don't remember most of it. I'd thought I'd been dreaming it all up until now. I'd like to see what is different from I remember."

The twins did their silent stare of communication before Carban nodded. "Very well. We have time before the wedding. However, you have to do what we say. Stay at our sides at all time. Understood?"

I eagerly bobbed my head.

"In any case," Coby's eyes crinkled at the corners and he wagged his eyebrows at me, "it will give me more chances to convince you to kiss me."

Letting out a grateful sigh, I released the key and brushed my hair behind my ear. "You are wasting your breath."

Coby tweaked my nose and winked. "Not a waste, if I win." He took a hold of my elbow and led me around the courtyard away from the door and to the archway guarded by two golden soldiers. Carban trailed after us, a pensive expression on his face. When the guards glanced our way, the twins merely inclined their heads, and the warriors let us be on our way.

Outside of the courtyard lay a dark and creepy set of woods. You couldn't see the ground because of the rolling fog. It stopped a few feet from the edge of the woods and seemed unable to go any further. Besides the ominous feeling, the wood gave off the sounds from inside that weren't any better. Manic laughter mixed with animals sounds, owls hooting, and wolves howling made my skin prickle and hair stand on end.

"We have to go in there?" I gulped, having second thoughts. The two-headed bird couldn't be worse than this. If I apologized, maybe they would forgive me and not bite my head off.

"I told you it was a dangerous trip," Coby said into my ear, closer than before which caused me to jump in place. "Are you sure you wouldn't rather go the short way around?"

I shook my head profusely. "No, no. This is fine. It'll be fine." I didn't know if I was trying to convince them or me.

"Alright, enough chit chat." Carban ran a hand through his hair, trying to rearrange it, but it simply settled back where it was before. "The queen will be expecting us to report back to her before long. I don't know about you, but I prefer my head where it is." He pushed away from us and headed toward the fog-covered woods.

"Hold on, Carban," Coby reached a hand out toward him and then paused and grabbed my hand, jerking me to his side. "Stay beside me and do not let go of my hand."

I nodded dumbly, more than happy to stay with him. Who knew what lay in the woods ahead of us?

We caught up to Carban who didn't give us a second thought. The twins didn't hold hands, not like how Coby had instructed me to. For a moment, I thought it might all be to reassure me, but then a loud growl rumbled through the trees, shocking birds from their nests and the ever-present laughter to cease briefly.

I clutched Coby's arm, my face pressed into his flexing bicep. The scent of his skin filled my nose, and for a moment, I forgot about my fear and a throbbing ache filled me.

"Oh," I breathed out, earning me a look from the owner of the arm.

"I wouldn't sniff me too much, Ally dear." He gently moved my face from his arm. "Humans aren't meant to be with us for too long. We've been known to be addicting."

I blinked rapidly and shook my head, breathing in and out to get rid of his scent from my nostrils. When I could finally think for myself once more, annoyance pinched my face. "Thank you for waiting until now to tell me."

Coby winked. "I could have used it to my advantage and gotten that kiss I've been wanting, but I didn't."

Rolling my eyes, I pursed my lips. "How gentlemanly of you."

"Quiet." Carban held a hand up, stopping us in our tracks. He turned his head this way and that, listening. When there was not a follow-up to the growl, he lowered his hand. "Come along. Let's get through here before whoever that was decided we would be good to have for lunch."

We continued through the woods, our steps a bit quicker than before. The ground beneath our shoes squished unpleasantly which made me grimace. I was glad for the fog, hiding what I might be stepping on. It wasn't surprising when the trees around us transformed into large mushrooms.

"Those weren't here before," Carban murmured, giving his brother a worried glance before moving more cautiously.

I stared up at the multicolored mushrooms surrounding us. Some were large as trees, others small as a child. They stood silently watching us as we moved through their little village. The fog had left us at the trees and I could now see the bright green grass beneath my feet. I didn't know why they were so upset about the mushrooms. I'd much rather be there than back in the woods. At least, it smelled better.

Opening my mouth to ask as much, a coughing fit came over me. Blue smoke wafted through the area and filled the air with clouds of it. The twins weren't bothered by the smoke. In fact, the appearance of it seemed to relax them. Coby even released my hand.

"You'd think he'd be a bit subtler," Carban groused, his eyes moving around the mushrooms. "Wouldn't it have been easier to send a message then uproot the whole fucking village?"

I waved my hand in front of my face, my nose crinkling at the sickly sweet smell. "Who?"

"Manciple," Carban said over his shoulder and then let out a pained sound. "I mean, Seer."

"It's Francis now, actually," a low humming voice corrected Carban.

Our heads turned toward the sound to see a blue man with a large stomach wrapped in a fuzzy dark blue coat lounging with a hookah pipe in between his lips. His black eyes rolled in his wrinkled face, barely paying us any mind at all.

"Preparing for the change?" Coby asked with an arch brow. "You don't look like a Francis."

We moved in closer, stopping right before the low mushroom the man was lying on. One white hand lifted from his lap and took the pipe from his lips. "You don't look like someone who has a hard time getting a woman to kiss him and yet here we are." He gave a condescending smile, and all six of his hands opened out to his sides.

My eyes did a double take. Six hands. What kind of Fae was this Seer person?

Taking the initiative, I stepped away from Coby and held my hand out. "Hello, I'm Al -

Ally." I shot a look at Coby who didn't offer me any directions.

Francis took my hand in one of his and brought it to his mouth, kissing it. "Well, now. You are quite a bit more put together than I expected you to be, Alice. Last I saw, you were still thinking you were in Wonderland. Better now?"

I flushed and ducked my head. "Yes, things have cleared up a bit for me. The Tweedles," Coby groaned at the word, "said you told them I was coming?"

"Ah, yes." Francis sucked on the end of his pipe and blew the smoke out in my direction. I turned my head and tried not to breathe it in. "I saw you coming and going. This time will be the last time, I'm afraid, at least for a while. You've got quite a journey ahead of you, so You should savor the moments you have now while they last." He angled his head toward the twins like he knew something I didn't. As a Seer, I supposed he did.

"So, what's with the theatrics?" Coby asked, waving a hand around and then reaching for the pipe. "Are you so weak you couldn't wait until we headed your way?"

Francis gave Coby a death glare and smacked his hand away. "Get your own. And I'm not weak. I'm simply conserving my energy." He shifted in his seat, drawing his coat closer to him. "The change always takes the majority of my strength, so I need reserves to keep myself safe during that time. You never know who's lying in wait for me to let my guard down." His large black eyes shifted around as if someone was waiting to jump him.

"I know how you feel." Carban shifted in place, visibly uncomfortable. "It's like eyes are watching me everywhere I go."

My eyes shot to the dark edges of the mushroom village. What were they talking about? Who was waiting to attack them?

"You best be on your way." Francis took a large puff of his pipe and then pointed it behind us. "There are so many left to meet and so little time. Best not waste it with me." I glanced behind us toward the way we came and then back to Francis who was barely visible now through all the smoke. "And Alice?"

"Yes?" I coughed and waved a hand in front of my face, trying to see him through the cloud.

"When we meet again, please do not be alarmed. Change is coming for all of us, even you."

With those mysterious last words, the smoke surrounded us, and it became difficult to breathe. I squinted and covered my mouth, trying to find the twins who had disappeared in the smoke. Taking a step away from where Francis sat and toward Coby, my foot caught on something. My hands went out trying to grab one of the twins before I went down but found only air.

My heart jumped into my throat as I braced for impact. The ground bit into my hands as they hit the dirt. A branch caught the side of my face, scratching my cheek and bringing tears to my eyes.

I lay on the ground for a few moments, giving into the despair of my situation. I could be getting married right now. Sure, the man was a complete cad, a total fake, but I could learn to love him or, well, like him. The big concern was convincing him not to divorce me or send me away.

"What ye be doin' down there?"

I looked up from my place on the ground toward the grumpy sounding voice above me. A little brown man with a pointed red hat and matching overalls leaned over me. He had a large nose and even bigger ears that almost consumed his small face. The beard along his chin was short and as dark as his onyx-colored eyes, which glared down at me.

"Well? Ye just gonna stare at me, girl?" He placed his fists on his hips and frowned further. "This ain't no place for a little thing like ye to be sleepin'."

Scrambling to my feet, I realized the little man only reached my waist. "I wasn't sleeping. I tripped." I paused and then my eyes widened. Turning around in a circle, my eyes searching for the twins and the mushroom village, but I saw nothing of the sort.

I gasped. "What? What happened? Where am I? Where's the Tweedles?"

"Tweedles? No Tweedles, only me. Bernard. Or, well... Mop as the case be." He rolled his dark eyes and scowled. "And ye be here with me. Where else might ye be?"

"But they were just here," I insisted in a squeaky, fear-riddled voice. "I had let go of Coby's hand for a just a moment and then I fell." I pointed at the ground, my lips tipping down.

"Those two pin-brain dummies haven't been here for ages," the little man huffed. "I don't see nobody but you, girl."

"Alice," I corrected him, only half paying him any mind, still searching for the twins who couldn't have just disappeared into thin air.

"Well, whatever your name be, if ye aren't where ye were before, then ye be truly lost. It happens here in Tundrey Woods."

109

"Tundrey Woods? That's where we are?" I cupped my elbow with my hand, bringing my hand up to my mouth so I could worry the nail. "How do I find them then?"

Mop lifted his small shoulders and shook his head, starting to leave me behind. "If ye be lost, then ye have to wait to be found. Lest ye know the way out?"

I chased after him. "Well, do you?"

"Do I what?" Mop glanced over his shoulder before stopping before a hole in a tree. He shoved whatever was in the hole around and threw a few items out, a book, a stuffed teddy, and a stool. A moment later, he scrambled inside himself and continued his search. Finally, he popped his head out of the hole.

"Aha!" He held up a large object almost twice his size. "Here be what we need, a lantern."

"I can see what it is." I put my hands on my hips and tapped my foot. "What I want to know is if you can help me get out of this place?" A bout of laughter came from behind the trees, sounding even more crazed than before. My shoulders bunched around my ears, and I searched the darkness. "What was that?"

"Where we be goin' next."

"What? Why?" He moved toward the sound of the laughter as he lit the lantern, and I reluctantly followed him. "I need to find the Tweedles. not some crazies who may or may not eat me." I startled at another round of laughter, not wanting to go any further.

"Keep up, girl, else ye be lost again. Ye don't know who might be findin' ye this time." He waved a hand over his shoulder, urging me to hurry up.

I sighed and gazed longingly around me as if that would bring the twins back out. Unfortunately, all that was there was the little brown creature called Mop and the cackling before me. Neither were very reassuring.

CHAPTER

FOLLOWING AS CLOSE TO Mop as I could, my anxiety increased with each step closer to the laughter. Mop waved a hand over his shoulder, "Come on, girl. This way."

When we pushed through the bushes, the laughter stopped. The silence was deafening. My heart rammed against my ribs as I took in the scene before me. Though the rest of the woods was covered in a dense fog, it cut off right at the edge of the clearing where a dimly lit table sat, much like it had at the Seelie palace. Eight chairs surrounded the table, each mismatched and out of place in the middle of a dark forest.

"This be as far as I go, girl." Mop stopped next to the head of the table, between an opalaught similar to Watch save for the bloodshot eyes and red-tinged fur and a tall-backed chair. "Hatter will watch ye while ye wait for those dummies to catch up."

"Please, brownie," a smooth rumbling voice announced as a pale finger tapped on the chair's arm. "You know how I abhor being referred to that name. It's Mercury or Merc. Nothing more."

Mop huffed. "It not be me who wants to call ye that. All this no-name nonsense be drivin' me batty." A sound came from a large bat creature with sparkling wings at the other end of the table, making Mop pause. "Apologies, Twinkle, but ye know what I mean."

"Unfortunately, I do." Mercury blew out a frustrated breath and then waved a hand from his chair. "Well, do not stand there all day. You are just in time for tea."

The opalaught laughed and cocked his head to the side, staring with wide eyes at the cup in his paw. The bat, Twinkle, cackled along with a large mouse the size of a dog with a large blue door covering his front. The mouse banged on the door and then coughed, his eyes twinkling with amusement.

I slowly approached the table covered in tea cups and plates of strange foods. A pot steaming from the middle of the table had the majority of the occupant's attention. I stopped beside the table where the mysterious Hatter poised in his chair. Long silver hair fell over his shoulders underneath a top hat. It was made of a dark blue material covered in patches and lined with a red ribbon that leaned over his face, hiding all but one stormy gray eye, while thin lips curled into a mischievous smile.

Mop shifted to the side so I could take his place, seeming more than happy to be rid of me. I turned my eyes from Mercury for a moment to see Mop grab his lantern and disappear back into the woods.

"Wait," I called out to him, moving away from the table and its insane-looking occupants, but Hatter's hand latched onto my wrist and pulled me down into his lap.

"Unhand me, sir." I fought against him, trying to get back onto my feet.

"Now, now. Relax. I'm not going to bite."

I stopped fighting long enough to peer underneath the hat. With the weight of both of those stormy grey eyes on me, I forgot how to speak. That mouth which had sounded so crazed curled, its owner as pleasantly surprised as I was. With a soft tug on my wrists, he brought my hands down to his chest where he wore a red and blue three-piece suit to match his hat. The body beneath hard and lean, the scent of him wafting from his skin and making my eyelids dip.

"You smell so..." I drew out, licking my lips as my body heated. I shifted, my thighs pressing together to relieve the ache there.

"Oh, a human," Hatter breathed, an elegant brow arching up to his hat. "How unexpected. How did a pretty thing like you find your way all the way here?" He pinched my chin between his fingers and leaned forward. Right when I thought he would kiss me, Hatter turned my face to the side, running his nose along my cheek as he inhaled. "Seelie. Who have you been playing with my dear?"

Half drunk on his scent, I wiggled in his lap needing to be closer. "The twins. Tweedles. The queen and Francis. I mean, Manciple. Wait." I shook my head, getting confused. "I mean, Seer? It's all very..." I shifted closer to him, burying my face in his hair. "... unimportant."

Hatter's hand sat on my lap as he pulled me closer to him but not touching me how I needed to be touched. I slid a hand underneath the neck of his shirt and the other tangled in his hair, my mouth finding the line of his jaw. A low rumble vibrated through him and along my form before he pushed me back slightly.

115

Those stormy grey eyes stared at me hard enough for me to blush.

"Why, good sir, do you see something you like?" I trailed my fingers along the line of my bodice, pushing my breasts up against the corset. His eyes dipped down briefly before meeting my eyes once more.

"While I would love nothing more than to take advantage of..." His hand cupped my thigh, pushing the skirt up so he could feel the skin beneath. My legs parted for him against my own volition. ",,, well, everything, the brownie wouldn't have left you here with me without a reason."

"A present?" the hare tittered behind me.

The bat looked up from his tea cup long enough to add, "A food present?"

"No, a used present," the mouse chimed in, leering at me.

I'd have been offended except my senses were so overwhelmed by the scent of the Fae holding me that they could have said anything, and I would have been okay with it.

"Hush now," Hatter chastised the others and then slid me to the ground as he stood from his chair. My front brushed against his as my feet hit the ground. Delicious ripples raced through me and I was more than ready for him to do whatever he liked with me.

116

Taking my hand, he led me away around the table and pulled out a seat two seats away from him. He gestured a hand toward the seat, and I happily took it. Pushing it in behind me, he offered me a cup, but the liquid he poured in was not from the pot in the middle of the table but from a flask in his jacket pocket.

"Drink up, love." He pushed the cup toward me. I lifted the chipped cup up to my lips and swallowed the bitter liquid, my eyes on him the entire time. "That's it. All of it. There's a girl."

The effects of the drink hit me before it settled in my stomach. My eyes cleared of lust, and my mind started to catch up to what was happening.

"Oh, my Lord," I gasped and glanced to him and then back to the table around me. I shifted away from him, suddenly feeling underdressed. "I... uh... I apologize. I didn't mean to accost you in such a manner."

Hatter moved away from me and took his seat once more, waving me off. "Never matter. A hazard of being a human in a Fae world. Now," he cleared his throat and laced his fingers in front of him, his stormy grey eyes locking onto me, "why don't we start over? Why don't we start with a name?" He opened his hands with the question.

I sat back in my seat, still a bit flushed and muttered, "Alice. Alice Liddell."

Recognition swept through Hatter's eyes and he leaned back in his chair. "You have grown much since I saw you last." His eyes roved over my form, letting me know just how much he liked how I'd grown. This time, the warmth I felt was completely from the intensity of his gaze and not his Fae tricks.

"My apologies, I don't remember." I lifted a shoulder. "Not much in any case."

"Understandable." Hatter inclined his head and exchanged a creepy smile with his fellow tea drinkers. "We know a thing or two about forgetting."

"Forget or forget not, who cares as long as they stir the pot." The opalaught cackled and threw himself around wildly in his chair.

Twinkle lifted his cup in the air as if giving a toast. "The pot do not. Stir the pot. If not, then the pot be stirred itself."

"What?" My mouth dropped open and my brows furrowed.

"The tea is ready." The mouse with a door on his chest gestured a clawed paw at the tea pot in the middle of the table. All three of them stared longingly at the pot, but none of them moved to pour the tea.

Turning my attention back to Hatter, I asked, "Do you know the Tweedles? I mean,

Coby and Carban? They were here with me, but then I got a bit lost." I glanced around us, hoping to see the mushrooms or even the twins magically back. It was Wonderland after all. It wasn't unheard of.

"I know of the Needle Twins, but I wouldn't call them Tweedles. They hate that." Hatter frowned. "I'm surprised they let you."

I lifted a shoulder. "Maybe I have grown on them."

With that, Hatter smiled. "I could certainly believe that." He stood once more, reaching across the table to pick up the tea pot.

The three others watched him with unnerving intent. I'd seen that kind of look before. Opiate addicts had that same strung-out bloodshot look about them. My mother and brother would be appalled to know I'd seen them, but Rhoda sometimes let me come with her to the apothecary, and I'd see them there begging for the doctor to give them more medicine. He'd send them away with a warning to get help before they killed themselves. It was one reason I'd never put much faith into concoctions. Healthy eating and daily walks around the park had kept me from falling ill on many of occasion.

"Since we have some time," Hatter continued, pouring a cup for himself but not passing the pot, "why don't you regale me with your adventures since you were here last? I'd much like to know where you have been and where you are going."

"Better for eating," the opalaught snapped, his eyes on the tea pot as his body shuddered.

"Eat. Eat. Yes. Eat," the mouse chanted, picking up a fork and knife.

Twinkle didn't add to the conversation this time but tapped his tea cup on the table insistently. Apparently, I did not rate higher than the tea.

Jerking my horrified gaze back to Hatter, I was happy to see he wasn't smiling. Waving a finger at him while holding the tea pot high up in the air, he said, "Now, now, Hare, Doormouse. Eating will be had, but not by you." Then he tilted his head to the side so his hair fell like a waterfall over his shoulder and offered me the pot. "Now, Alice, would you like a cup?"

CHAPTER

I STARED DOWN INTO my cup as if the leaves inside might give me some kind of answer to my conundrum. I'd never expected to be in Wonderland of all places, but here I was, sitting at Hatter's table drinking his tea.

Things had certainly gotten out of control. When I'd followed that would-be rabbit, I'd expected to corner the thing and figure out why he was following me, but that didn't exactly happen. I still hadn't found Watch. I'd committed a crime by stealing the Between key, and now, I was waiting for two men I barely knew to come rescue me from the clutches of the most deliciously handsome man I'd ever met.

If that didn't make matters worse, I found myself attracted to not just the Fae before me but the twins as well. I'd never been so interested in the opposite sex in all my twenty years. Lewis had been the first one who'd ever even peaked my interest and look how that turned out.

Now, I had so many choices before me and no answers in sight. Did I go back to Lewis? Could I stay here? Or maybe there was something else out there for me entirely?

I let out a dejected breath of air and dropped my cup on the table.

"What could ever be so wrong, dear Alice? You never drink my tea." I glanced up from my cup long enough to see Hatter's eyes. They had turned silver from the effects of the tea and narrowed over the edge of his cup.

"Nothing." Letting out a melancholy sigh, I leaned back in my seat. The only ones left were Hatter and me. The Hare, the Doormouse, and even Twinkle had long gone to bed. Well, when I say bed, I meant that they were passed out in various locations around the table. I was pretty sure the feet sticking out from beneath the blood red table cloth belonged to Twinkle, the cheerful little bat. No one left was cheerful.

Hatter sat his cup down. The sound of it clinking against its dish made Hare snort in his sleep, one ragged ear flopped over his face as he rolled over. I huffed a smile.

Letting out a dark chuckle, Hatter rolled his head around, getting the kinks out. "Now, that's a lot of nonsense if I ever heard any. Nothing? There's no such thing as nothing because there is always something. And if there's always something, then the thoughts twisting around in that pretty head of yours are hardly nothing."

His tidbit of nonsense actually made quite a lot of sense for once. However, it wasn't enough to make me spill my secrets to the gorgeous mad man. Not so easily.

"Have you ever been in love?" I asked, pouring myself another cup of tea. I'd learned quite quickly that Hatter was the only one allowed to pour the tea. The others almost bit my hand off when I had tried. However, now they were asleep, and Hatter seemed perfectly content to let me serve myself.

I lifted the cup to my lips, letting the warm, bitter yet fruity liquid fill me and settle in my stomach. Each sip made my head foggy, and those oh so troublesome thoughts floated away. I could see how they could become addicted.

Hatter smiled deviously. "Of course I have. One should fall in love often. No less than twice a week, at least that's what I always say."

Frowning at him, I placed my elbow on the table and put my face on my palm. If my mother saw me, how she would have fainted out of pure embarrassment. However, she was not here, so her nagging at my manners were a moot point. Hatter, on the other hand, was and had brought up a very interesting question.

"Fall in love? Twice a week? What of marriage?"

Hatter ran his fingers through his long silky hair and winked lazily at me. "If one must, but I never seen the worry about a piece of paper. It's not a magic spell that keeps those we love from betraying us or leaving." He spoke as if he were an expert on the topic, and for all I knew, he might be.

I sniffed and shifted in my seat. "Quite right."

Hatter pushed back from the table, adjusting his red waist coat and blue jacket as he waltzed over to where I sat. His fingers trailed along the table top, his eyes locked onto me as he moved. Stopping at my side, he leaned a hip against the table. Curious eyes stared down at me, making me squirm.

Maybe it was the tea or maybe it was just Hatter himself, Fae tricks and all, but my mouth watered, and my blood pulsed between my thighs at the scent of him this close. It was a mixture of tobacco, tea leaves, and something that was completely him. Lewis never caused such a reaction in me, no matter how much he made me feel wanted before his slip up.

"What makes this Alice think of marriage? Have a manly caller waiting for your hand?" Hatter brushed a strand of my blonde hair back and behind my ear, his fingers tingling as they traced the edge of my face.

Ducking my head to hide my wanton expression, I fiddled with my tea cup. "I'm engaged, practically married already, to a man who I have just recently discovered has been using me for my tales of Wonderland" - my gaze jerked up to see Hatter's eyes burning with fury - "to write a bloody fucking book!"

Hatter did not reprimand me for speaking of my fiancé in such a manner or for cursing. I could blame the twins' influence, but really, it was my own fault. My own anger billowed up and fell out of my mouth before I could think better of it.

Hatter didn't seem to mind though, not as my family would have. However, Hatter's actions were much worse. Reputation ruining, even. Well, not that those mattered here.

"No man in their right mind would use a woman for such a frivolous thing. If you were mine..." His hand cupped my chin, lifting it as his face lowered, his breath hot against my lips. I could smell the tea on his breath, and it only made me want him more.

"If you were mine," he reiterated, "I'd splay you across my table while I ravished you. Nothing is sweeter and gives a greater high than what lies between those milky thighs." His eyes dipped down to my lap as if he could see through the very clothes I wore.

His gaze and his words burned me to the core, and my thighs slid against each other, viciously trying to subdue the wanton need there. Now, I knew the tea was beginning to work because I wasn't quite so outraged as I should be, could be, oh, there's the rhyming again, and I could only think of one thing to say in return to Hatter's salacious words.

"I wish you would."

Those silver eyes darkened, and his hand appeared in front of me. I didn't even hesitate before my palm slid into his warm one. He hauled me to my feet and spun us around. My back hit the table, and then his hands were on my hips, lifting me up and onto the table. My breath came out quickly now having never done anything like this before.

Carban had been my first kiss, for goodness' sake.

"Breathe," Hatter murmured, taking my face in between his hands. "Just breathe." His face came closer to mine and my eyelashes fluttered closed, my lips parted in anticipation of his kiss.

That never came.

Hatter's nose brushed along my cheek and nose, the barest of touches. One hand released my face and cupped the back of my neck, tilting my head back. His mouth dropped to my neck, where he placed hot, open mouth kiss against my pulse, sucking on the skin there.

My mouth dropped open, and I gasped at the sensation. My legs spread of their own accord allowing Hatter to move in closer to me. I didn't care that we weren't alone or that the twins could show up at any moment. The only thing that mattered was what Hatter offered.

I'd long since stopped believing that I cared anything for Lewis other than being a way out of my brother's house and my family's hair. Now that I knew he was nothing but a filthy liar, I didn't care one inch about what he might think or feel. As far as I was concerned, the marriage wasn't going to happen. Not now. Not ever.

"Stop thinking, dear Alice." Hatter lifted his head from my neck, his eyes locking onto mine. "Let me take care of you as I always promised I would."

This time when he leaned in, his mouth pressed to mine. My hands lifted off the table and tangled into his hair, much like how our tongues tangled together. Hatter tasted of tea and dark promises, ones I'd forgotten about until his mouth touched mine.

"Will you marry me, Mr. Hatter?" a child version of myself innocently asked to the older man, grinning behind her tea cup.

"Marriage? Why would you think of such a thing, little one?" Hatter grinned at me as his friends laughed. "And please, call me Mercury for the last time. Hatter is my profession, not my name." He sniffed, adjusting his tie.

Giggling at his strange behavior, the younger me shook her head. "Everyone gets married. My mother said so. She said I'd have to get married when I was older and that I should forget all my make-believe nonsense, but you're not make believe. You're right here."

"Quite right, I am." Hatter inclined his head with a superior sniff. "And as for marriage, I never marry my betters. You will need to grow a few feet and sin a time or two before I could ever consider tying the knot."

"Promise?"

"Have I ever lied?" Hatter arched a brow, and Hare made a disbelieving sound, sending a cup flying through the air. The memory ended with us laughing and spilling tea everywhere.

I pulled back from Hatter with a gasp. Hatter stared at me with curious eyes as I traced the lines of his face with my fingertips. "Have I sinned enough for you, Mercury? Or am I still your better?"

A pleased sort of expression crossed his face, and his hands slid underneath my skirt, wrapping around my thighs. He dragged me across the table, pressing his hard length against the apex of my thighs.

"Oh, Alice. You will always be the better of us, except now I have no reason to not keep my promise."

My skirt bunched up at my hips as he kissed me once more, his fingers finding the undergarments the twins had given me. Releasing my lips, he dragged them down, and I lifted my hips allowing him to take them off. He brought them up to his face, breathing them in as he met my gaze.

"I'll just put these somewhere safe." He smirked and tucked them into the pocket of his jacket.

My hands dropped back down to the table, and I leaned back in anticipation. Warm calloused hands moved up the top of my thighs, thumbs pressing on the insides and urging me to open my legs further. Hatter suddenly shot forward and kissed me so deeply that I felt it in my toes, but then, just as quick as it happened, he released me.

With a wicked flash of his teeth, he dropped down before me. I watched him intently, unsure but exhilarated to find out what he was going to do. His breath teased long my skin, and he pressed a kissed to the inside of my thigh and then the same thing to the other one. My core pulsated for attention.

The first swipe of his tongue made my hips jump off the table, causing him to chuckle. The laugh reverberated through my heat, and I let out a needy moan. Not waiting for me to prepare, he kissed between my legs the same way he had kissed my mouth not a few moments ago. My eyelids squeezed shut, my mind completely going blank from the intense pleasure Hatter was inducing.

"Don't mind us," Coby snapped, my eyes flying open to see him and Carban standing a few feet away. "We've just been searching all over Tundrey Woods for you."

I gasped as Hatter flicked his tongue against me, and I pulled on his hair, trying to get him to stop. "Hatter. Hatter. The twins. They're... ah!" I cried out, my mouth falling open and a low moan ripping through me, the hand on his head no longer trying to stop him but push him closer. My body shuddered and relented to Hatter's ministrations despite the twins watching us. "Oh, Lord. Oh, God. I'm... ah... Mercury!"

While I tried to recover, Hatter stood and drew my dress back down. He turned slightly, pulled a handkerchief from his jacket pocket, and wiped the sides of his lips. "Ah, my apologies. I didn't know we had company. Please, have some tea."

I let out a shuddering laugh and fell back on the table with a winced. "Ouch." I reached behind my back and grabbed the thing that had stabbed me. Lifting it up, I gave the twins an ironic grin. "Fork."

CHAPTER

CARBAN STARED AT ME as if he were just seeing me for the first time, kind of like he did right after he had kissed me. It made me feel pleased and exposed all at the same time.

I shifted off the edge of the table and pulled my skirt down over my legs. "Where have you been?"

Coby snorted. "Like you care?" He gestured a hand between Hatter and me. "Here I've been, trying to get a lowly kiss, and Merc gets all the goods."

Mercury let out a pleased chuckle, wrapping his arm around my waist. "What can I say? You just don't have what it takes to satisfy my girl."

His hand caressed my face before I pushed him away with a scowl. "Stop gloating. I'm mad at you." When he only laughed, I smacked him on the arm. "It's not funny."

"My apologies, my love." Hatter captured my hand before I could hit him again, pressing it to his mouth. "You just taste so good. I couldn't stop."

I rolled my eyes, fixing my hair and moving toward the twins. "Please ignore him. He's had too much tea."

Carban nodded stiffly but Coby gave me a longing sigh. "I really was looking for you too. When the smoke covered us, I couldn't find you, and then, the next thing I know, I'm back in the woods and some little brown man named Mop is leading me here."

"Mop." Hatter supplied with a wink and a salacious slide of his tongue across his teeth. "The brownie."

My forehead scrunched down at the word but then shrugged. Better to know what he was then keep calling him the little man. "Anyway, I've been waiting for you here, but now that you're here, we can go."

"Are you sure you don't just want to stay here with Mercury?" Carban cocked his head to the side, a bit of a bite to his words. "You seemed more comfortable with him."

Oh, my. Was Carban jealous? It flattered me and confused me at the same time. Sure, we'd kissed, but I had thought it to be for the sake of the guards. Did he truly think it meant more?

Before I had a chance to ask him, Coby nudged his brother in the ribs. "Why are you complaining? At least you got to kiss her. I've gotten jack squat. Coby swaggered over to me, lacing his fingers with mine and bringing them up to his lips. "Though I'm a forgiving Fae after all."

Flushing and giggling at his teasing, I withdrew my hand from him and patted him on the cheek. "When you do something worth earning a kiss, then perhaps you will receive one."

Coby gaped and pointed at his brother. "He didn't do anything to deserve his kiss. What about him?"

I lifted a nonchalant shoulder. "That was different. Life or death situations are the exception."

Letting out a disgusted snort, Carban crossed his arms over his chest, giving a pointed look at Hatter. "You must have been in real turmoil then."

Pursing my lips, I placed my fists on my hips. "That was different as well. We've met before and..." I was going to blame it on the tea, but I knew very well what I had been doing and did it, anyway. "Mercury and I..."

"We're engaged," Hatter supplied, wrapping a happy arm around my shoulders.

"Again?" Coby gaffed. "Isn't one fiancé enough for you?"

I lifted a finger and shook my head. "Technically, Mercury and I were engaged before Lewis even knew I existed so that predates. It cannot be helped that I didn't remember it."

"Sure, keep telling yourself that," Coby teased and then pulled on his pants and shifted in place. "Well, engaged or not. I still would like that kiss." He wagged his brows at me, and I laughed.

Carban only scowled harder.

"Well, I certainly do not object, but that would be up to my dear Alice." Hatter's arm wrapped around my shoulders, reached out, and cupped my face turning it up to him. He pressed his mouth mine, kissing me so deeply that my knees sagged beneath me. When he released me, we were both breathless. He traced the lines of my lips with a soft expression. "My heart has always been at her mercy, and any scrap of her love would be enough for me."

My face heated, and I swore it went down to my toes. No one had ever said such lovely words to me before. Lewis had definitely never expressed such love and devotion. I'd thought just having him listen to my ramblings was enough, but I'd been so very wrong.

"Enough about kissing and such things, or we'll never get out of here." Carban unfolded his arms and turned from the table, giving us his back. "Come or don't. I no longer care."

Discouraged by Carban's words, I glanced at Coby and Hatter before following after him. "I still have to help you with the wedding. I wanted to meet the princess and prince. Also, I..." My hand reached in my pocket where the key to the door leaving the Underground sat. "I need..."

"To get home." Hatter finished for me, a sad smile on his face. "I understand. It's not as if you could stay, anyway. Very well, I'll escort you. A fleeting love is better than none at all."

Before I could ask him what he meant, Hatter followed after Carban, leaving me and Coby. I turned my pleading gaze to him, begging him to understand or to explain. I wasn't sure which.

Coby shook his head, a forlorn emotion in his eyes. "You can't have it both ways, Ally." He patted me on the shoulder and then took my hand. "Keep close. This time, we may not be able to find you."

I clutched onto Coby's hand as if I might lose them at any moment. My mind and heart were at war with each other.

On one hand, I knew I needed to go home. I had people to answer to. Namely a wedding to cancel and a face to slap, that face being Lewis. Then I would be able to come back here and be with Hatter and the Twins.

The Twins. Where did they fit into my heart? I'd only just met them, and while I did tease Coby some, I did like them quite a bit. I couldn't see myself never seeing them again. Whether I would allow them as close as Hatter was another matter.

In the human world, one man married one woman, and that was the end of it. Many had lovers of course, but they were very hush hush or, if the public found out, quite frowned upon. Not that I ever really cared what society thought. I'd already destroyed any chances I had to fit in a long time ago.

So, what did it matter now if I choose to give my heart to more than one man? If I stayed in the Underground, no one back home would even know. They wouldn't be able to tell me it was wrong or too scandalous for polite society. I could have everything and not ever have to worry about what they thought again.

Then again...

What of my family? While my mother did frustrate me at times, she was still my mother. I couldn't completely write her off, could I? The same went for my siblings. I didn't want to forget about them, especially not Rhoda. She and I were two peas in a pod. We'd always been there for one another. I couldn't leave her to the world's cruel clutches. Perhaps I could take her with me. Bring her back here? Or even visit!

I'd come and gone before. Why should now be any different? Why couldn't I come back and forth like before?

Tired of my own inner fight, I asked as much.

Hatter turned from where he was whispering with Carban. "Things have changed quite a bit in the Underground from when you were a child, dear Alice. We do not have the freedom we once had."

"Why not?" I glanced down at Coby's hand, then to Hatter and reached a hand out. My heart hitched when he instantly slowed and took it. I started to release Coby's hand, but he held tight, raising a brow at me to argue. Not bothered by it, I allowed them both to hold my hand as we moved in step, only Carban slightly ahead.

"The woods here, for example," Hatter explained, gestured around us. "When you were a child, you were able to travel through it safely to me any time you wish. But now..." He moved his head from side to side. "Now, I'm surprised you didn't come across something even worse in their depths before you came across Mop."

I thought for a moment and then asked, "Does it have something to do with these new names?" Carban peeked over his shoulder at me at my question. "I couldn't help but notice you all seem to be conflicted about what to call you. Hatter. Mercury. Tweedles. Coby. Carban. Even this Mop character. Why are you using fake names?"

"The Shadows."

I stopped in my tracks at the new voice. The other three stopped as well, but they did not seem confused. I searched around for the owner of the voice and found a handsome man leaning against a new by tree. He watched us with growing interest.

Dark blue eyes peered out of an aristocratic face. Long black hair hung to his waist and was braided to show off his pointed ears where long blood red rubies hung. His simple black shirt opened at the collar and his matching pants were tucked into knee-high boots. While he didn't wear a crown or royal clothing like the king and queen of the

Seelie Court had, everything about him screamed important. Powerful.

"My prince." Hatter didn't release my hand as he dropped to a knee. Coby and Carban bowed as well but not as low at Hatter.

"Rise." The prince lifted a hand for Hatter to stand. "No need for such formalities here." He gave the twins a sardonic grin before turning his watchful eyes to me. "Alice Liddell, you have grown quite well."

"Uh... thank you, Your Highness. I would curtsy but..." I lifted my otherwise occupied hands with a sheepish baring of my teeth.

The prince gave me a curious look. "Why are you calling me Your Highness? You never do that."

My eyes widened. "Oh. We've met before?"

"Do you not remember?"

Hatter stepped forward, still holding my hand. "My apologies, Your Highness, but it seems our Alice has lost some of her memories. We have been collecting them." He gave me a secretive wink.

"Very well, then." The prince grinned. "I won't ruin it. Your Highness or Prince will do."

Not wanting to get detoured too much by the conversation, I asked, "And what of the Shadows?"

"Oh, yes." The prince moved from the tree and approached us. "There are a few in this world that do not follow the rules, and those who are deemed not fit to stay in our world are cast into the Shadow Realm. There they fester and fade until there is nothing more than a glimpse of themselves left." He frowned and rubbed his jaw line. "Unfortunately, it seems that some of them have escaped their prison and are wreaking havoc on both courts."

"They call you into the night by your name," Coby told me, whispering in my ear. "Only the strongest are able to break the seductive pull of their power. So, it is better to not let them know your name at all."

A chill went down my spine, and I hoped I'd never have to worry about resisting the call. I had enough on my plate without fretting over creatures I couldn't see or resist. If the Fae were scared, then I doubted a human would be able to do anything against it.

"Perhaps, I should have a name as well." I shot a look around the group. "For my own protection, of course."

The prince laughed. "Well, it wouldn't hurt, but seeing as you can't stay here for longer than a few days at a time, I think you might be alright."

141

That was the second time someone said I couldn't stay. It was beginning to put a chip in my overall plan.

"Why can't I stay?"

No one answered for a moment. Hatter broke the silence first.

"Humans and Fae age very differently, my love." His beautiful lips curved downward, and pain filled his eyes. "Our world does not run on the same time as yours. You might be alright for now, but after a prolonged amount of time in our world..." He trailed off as if he couldn't bear to tell me.

"You'd die," Carban said from a few steps away, and my head jerked in his direction. His face was stony as he spoke, no emotion in his voice what so ever. "Your internal clock would shift to match ours and then you would age normally in your world here. Your minutes would turn to seconds. Your days to years. And then," he snapped his fingers, "like that. You're gone."

CHAPTER

AFTER CARBAN'S HEAVY REVELATION, I should have had a moment to think, to re-evaluate what I was doing and where I was going. Sadly, lady luck was not on my side.

No sooner had he said it, then a buzzing sound came toward us at a rapid pace.

"What is that?" I glanced around the woods, trying to find the source of the sound.

It took a moment before the prince cursed. "Faeries. Fucking faeries."

The men tensed at the prince's revelation and then, as if someone had signaled them, they broke out into a run. Coby released my hand, allowing Hatter to take me with him as we ran.

Over rocks and branches, broken tree trunks, and around large bushes we ran while the buzzing increased even quicker now. First, Carban went missing in the fog and then Coby. The prince had long disappeared with a flap of wings and an owl hoot. Only Hatter and I remained, and even that didn't last long.

"Oomph," I gasped as I tripped and hit the ground, my hand leaving Hatter's. In what felt like slow motion, Hatter turned to help me up but was swarmed by a pack of little bug-like creatures. I cried out and scrambled to my feet, but the moment I stood up, a part of the pack broke away from Hatter and came after me.

Not wanting to leave Hatter but also not wanting to die, I tried to lead the pack away, swatting at them as they nipped at me. "You nasty little buggers. Leave me alone." My eyes were closed tightly so I couldn't tell where I was headed, only that I couldn't hear Hatter or the woods anymore.

With a cackling wail, the insect-sized faeries dove at my legs, knocking me off my feet once more. I hissed as the ground scratched my hands when I landed in the gravel and dirt. At this rate, I'd have no skin left on my hands.

I threw my arms over my head without the chance to check out my injuries as I anticipated the next round of attacks. However, it didn't come. Slowly, I removed my hands and peeked up from the ground. They were gone.

Sighing, I moved to my knees and glanced at my hands. The cuts weren't as bad as I had expected. Only the top skin had been damaged. I'd have to get them cleaned as soon as I could though.

Looking up from my stinging hands, I searched for the faeries or even the slightest hint of where I was or where my companions had gone. Nothing. I recognized nothing.

To the front of me, dead grass and dirt patches pitted the ground. There was more rock than plants, and though there were trees and bushes, they were bare and twisted like they had been struck by lightning. It was as if all the life had been sucked out of the place, leaving nothing but a deserted wasteland behind.

Behind me sat the woods, in all their creepy darkness. Turning from the way I had obviously come, I stared down the path before me or what little there seemed to be of one. There was a weird light along the path even though the night sky was void of any kind of moon. I shivered at the ominous presence coming from the direction of the path. Did I really want to go it alone?

I could go back the way I came and hope that I ran into one of my companions, though they had warned me of going into the woods alone. There might be worse things in those trees than what I'd already met. Remembering the loud growl that had scared the birds from their trees made up my mind for me.

Sticking my hand in my pocket, I wrapped my fingers around the ribbon of the key, and made my way down the path, keeping a wary eye on the shadows in between the trees. Something made the faeries leave me alone. It couldn't have just been the horrible decor.

With each step I took, I was beginning to understand why.

I could feel eyes boring into me like an itch along my skin. I jumped when a branch near me snapped. My eyes darted to the sound as I searched around in the dim light for the culprit.

Finding nothing, I quickened my pace along the path. My feet moved even faster as more branches and twigs snapped beneath what sounded like little feet. Giggles echoed out in the dark at my rising fear.

I stumbled as a buzzing noise flew by, giving a vicious tug on my hair. I spun around, but nothing was behind me. There was more snickering, and then there was another yank on my hair from behind me.

"Leave me alone, you faeries. I know you're out there. Just leave me alone!" I stomped my foot. I heard tiny peals of laughter at my display of emotion. They were playing with me. Well, I would show them.

I listened for the telltale sound of their buzzing wings. When it came close to me, I threw my hand out and prayed I hit something. My hand hit something solid, and a squeak followed. I searched around me for what I hit before landing on a small moving figure on the ground.

Not more than four inches tall was a small stick. No. Not a small stick, it was a faerie. Its skin was brown and grey like the bark of a tree, its wings thin skeletal spines with barely enough skin covering them to allow flight.

I inched closer to get a better look at it. Its arms and legs were as skinny as its torso, which wasn't much bigger than my pinky. Its fingers were bone thin as were its toes, and its scowling face was as thin as the rest of it. It had long, wiry black hair and no clothes or any distinguishing gender parts. Razor-sharp teeth snarled at me, and its big black eyes bored a hole into my face.

I stuck a finger out toward it, and it gnashed its sharp little teeth at me. I jerked my hand back with a small scream, causing the winged creature to snicker.

Growling at my own cowardice, my hand shot out and snatched the little shit up. It waved its fists in alarm, its voice a high-pitched noise as it yelled profanities at me in a language I didn't understand. I brought the creature up to eye level and frowned.

"Could you calm down for a moment, please? You are throwing quite a fit, and I do not have time for you. I have to find my friends." I glared at the buzzing coming from the branches. Their little bodies and shiny black eyes became clear to see now that I knew what I was looking for. "Oh, hush now. You are worse than my little sister, and that is saying something."

I released the faerie, but my little speech had only antagonized it further. It sank its claw into my hand, and when I shook it, it bit me. With its teeth still in my hand, it grinned up at me. Tears filling my eyes, I struggled to get the creature to release me.

"Now that's not very nice. Let go." I grabbed its tiny body and tugged on it. It didn't so much as budge. Then I grabbed its wings. The moment my fingers took hold of them, it released my hand with a pop.

Then the horde hiding in the shadows decided they'd had enough waiting. They poured out of the trees and came after me. This time, I did the smart thing. I ran.

A hundred faeries chased after me, their little wings making that horrid buzzing sound as they flew. Thankful to not have a long skirt to hold me down, I raced down the pathway, searching for an end to the madness. After a few moments, my lungs began to burn, and my legs ached. I wasn't going to last much longer, and there was no end in sight.

What was I going to do? I couldn't die here. I had so much left to do. So many questions unanswered. My family would forever be searching for me with never getting an answer. Then there was Hatter and the twins. What would they do when they found me? Eaten to bits by faeries.

"Fucking faeries," I breathed out harshly and let out a laugh though it pained me to do so.

Then an unexpected sound of panic came from the horde, a collective cry of fear and outrage. I didn't dare pause to look back though, in case it was a trick.

A familiar voice reached my ear. "Alice. Alice, stop."

My footsteps slowed. My head turned slowly, and my eyes locked with Coby's at the same time I slammed into a hard body.

Letting out a hard breath, I grabbed onto whatever I'd run into to keep from falling as strong arms wrapped around my waist, drawing me closer.

The familiar scent of leather and musk filled my senses and my eyelids drooped. I peered up at Carban with a loopy smile. "Hello."

Carban's jaw clenched, and he released me. "You can stop running now. We got rid of them all."

"Oh, alright," I murmured, not moving away from him. I'd never realized how pretty his eyelashes were, how good he smelled. I wanted to rub my face against him like a cat.

All of a sudden, Carban pushed me away. I stumbled and almost fell. Shaking my head to clear it, I didn't chastise him for it. Slowly, twisting on my heel, I faced Coby.

"How did you get rid of them?"

"Fire." Coby held up a torch burning with a blue flame. "Reaper fire. A pain in the ass to get but it works every time."

"The Veil of the Faeries is the graveyard for dead Fae. The Reaper comes collecting every few days. Only he can keep those nasty bugs in line," Carban explained, moving to his brother's side. "We shouldn't dally here. They'll come back or worse... the Reaper will."

My mind whirled as I processed this latest bit of information, but before I could ask more questions, they were walking away. I scurried after them, reaching for Coby's hand.

"You don't need to hold my hand now, Ally." He paused and then gave me a flirty smile. "Not unless you want to of course."

I met his gaze and then, without really thinking about it, took his hand. "So, where to now?"

The twins exchanged a silent question and then Coby nodded. "The Cat's home isn't too far from here. We'll go there and then the palace. We can use his looking glass to skip the rest of the nonsense of this side."

"The cat? Where's Mercury? And what do you mean this side? Isn't your side this way too?" I asked, trying to keep pace with them as we headed down another path and what seemed to be back toward the woods.

Carban decided to speak to me this time. "Each court has their own dangers. We are better equipped to handle our own."

Squeezing my hand in reassurance, Coby said, "Hatter will meet us at the Cat's home. We've already sent him a message through the trees." He waved a hand around us as we stepped back into the woods for what I hoped would be the last time.

"And the cat?" I urged, wanting to know if the cat was the same one from my dreams, a cute little pink and purple ball of fuzz that rudely directed me through the forest.

"Cheshire will host us for a time, if he is so inclined." Coby gave me a lazy grin and then said nothing more about it.

CHAPTER

"IS IT MUCH FURTHER?" I gasped, my feet pulsating in my shoes. "We've been walking for hours."

"It hasn't been that long." Carban threw over his shoulder at my whining.

I made a whimpering sound, barely hanging onto Coby's hand. Carban huffed and, before I could say another word, scooped me up into his arms.

Letting out a small eep, I looped my arms around Carban's neck. His bright green eyes locked with mine, exasperation making his eyes roll. "Better?"

I shifted as I got used to his arms around me. With a soft sigh, I smiled. "Yes. Very. Thank you."

Coby chuckled. Coming up to his brother's side, he tickled my ankle. "If I'd known that the only thing I needed to do to get you in my arms was to offer you a lift, I'd have started with that."

I threw my head back and laughed, jiggling my foot out of his grasp. "Stop it, already. Just because Carban is carrying me doesn't mean I'm going to kiss him..." My words trailed off as my eyes met Carban's and then dipped down to his lips. My tongue darted out to wet my lips before I breathed, "... again."

Wrapped in his arms, his scent enveloping me, I found myself leaning up toward him. Carban's eyelids dipped, his mouth parting. My fingers curled in the nape of his neck as I lifted my face.

"We're here."

Coby's voice broke the spell, and Carban dropped my legs, pushing me away from him and into Coby's arms. Baffled by what had just happened, I clutched Coby's vest and watched Carban walk away from us and toward a clearing.

"See?" Coby groused. "He grumps and growls and almost gets a kiss. I have been nothing but lovely, and I don't get shit."

I sighed and patted Coby's chest. "I admit. I haven't been very fair to you. You have been perfectly lovely, especially compared to your brother."

"Too true." His full bottom lip poked out, and he looked so adorable pouting like a child.

Pulling my lower lip into my mouth as I fought back a smile, I lifted my finger up to his mouth. His lips parted, and his tongue darted out to taste me before he pulled my full finger into his mouth, snipping at it before sucking on the tip. A rush of emotion rolled through me, and I pressed up on my toes to replace my finger with my lips.

The hand on my waist moved to the back of my head, pressing me closer to him and his delectable mouth. Kissing him was nothing like kissing his brother. Where Carban had overwhelmed me with passion, Coby took his time.

His mouth brushed against mine, once, twice, and then three times. He teased my lips until I was begging for him to give me more. I clung to him, pressing my chest against him, pulling him until we were practically one.

"If you're done, the cat will receive us now," Carban growled, a bit more aggressive about it than was needed.

"My apologies, brother." Coby smirked, releasing my mouth and then tipping up my chin. "I got distracted." A matching grin on my lips, I couldn't get enough of him.

Rolling his eyes, Carban turned on his heels and marched back into the clearing, not waiting for us to follow. Giving Coby a small peck on the cheek, I took him by the hand and led him after his brother. "Come on."

The clearing itself was untouched by the fog which seemed to fill the rest of the forest. It cut off just at the tree line, creating a perfectly circular outline of milky white.

While the tea party had a sort of ominous lighting, in this clearing, it was like the clouds had opened up just enough to illuminate the area. In the middle, sparkling in the sunlight, was a large willow tree. Its long, fuchsia vines were covered in bright violet leaves. They hung all along each side and reached down to brush the ground.

I gaped at the vines, marveling at the sight before me. Carban pushed through the vines without a thought. The vines rippled and whispered, even though there was no wind to move them, and then the vines pulled back, opening like a curtain. A lone vine whipped inward as if to welcome us inside.

Coby and I moved into the depths of the trees, my eyes wandering about the tree, trying to catch everything. It was unlike anything I'd ever seen before. The sugar fairyland inside of the tree was out of place in the middle of the nightmare of a forest. It was almost a relief to see.

"Oh, my," I marveled, releasing Coby to turn around in place. "Are we dreaming?"

Chuckling at my actions, Coby rubbed his jaw. "The cat does have quite a thing for theatrics. The magic alone to create such a display is far more than most Fae are allowed."

"Uh huh," I murmured, my eyes still taking in the surroundings.

Luminescent, emerald green grass carpeted the ground and bounced beneath my feet. Every inch of the ground was covered in flowers of every hue and color. A path of grass lined by bright pink mushrooms trailed up from the willow vines to the base of the tree where a high-backed chair sat empty.

"Well, where is he?" I moved my head from side to side, my hands out to my side in dismay. "And where is Carban?"

"Inside," a rumbling bored voice answered from above.

My head tipped back, up the tree trunk to the branches above. Sitting on a branch sat a purple ball of fur. That cat!

"You again!" I pointed a finger at him, my eyes wide. "I should have known."

The purple ball uncurled, and a small cat head popped out, a curious sort of look on its face. "Yes, you should have."

Turning away from the cat, I glowered at Coby, gesturing a hand up to the cat. "What's this?"

"Alice, meet Cheshire." Coby tucked his hands into his pockets, rocking back and forward in place a twinkle in his eyes. "Our host and friend."

The cat hissed and lashed out a clawed paw. "I have not yet agreed to be your host, and I am certainly not your friend, Tweedle swat."

I stiffened at his insults and shot a nervous look at Coby, who didn't seem bothered by Cheshire's words in the slightest. To my surprise, he actually laughed and then waved a hand, gesturing for the cat to come down.

"Is the pretty pussy still mad that I beat him at cards?" Coby gave the cat a full tooth grin. "I'd think you'd have gotten over that a long while back. Come down, and next time you're in Summerville, I'll buy you a saucer of milk."

With an angry growl, the cat jumped from his perch. In mid-air, the tiny thing transformed into a tiger of purple and black strips. He barreled at Coby whose eyes

158

widened but didn't move fast enough to dodge the cat's attack.

Knocking Coby to the ground, Cheshire pressed a sharp-tipped paw on the twin's chest and peered down at him with blinking emerald green eyes.

"Who are you calling a pussy? I'll bite your cock off before I take anything from you." Cheshire licked his jaws and snapped his teeth in Coby's face but didn't aim to hurt the tailor, only scare him.

"Leave him alone," I snapped, taking a step toward the tiger, "you mangy beast!"

The tiger languidly turned his head from Coby to focus on me. Those eyes so large and brightly out of place in the tiger's head made me stumble back. Stupid Alice, threatening something bigger than you. Stupid, stupid girl.

"See, now you've gone and upset Ally." Coby sighed with distaste. "It's alright, Ally. He's just fucking around."

I frowned at his vulgar words but didn't stop staring at the tiger. He seemed to be studying me. His gaze moved along my body in a slow perusal. I couldn't tell what he was thinking behind those slanted pupils. For all I knew, he could be slowly planning how to eat me or worse maul me to death.

159

He broke his gaze away and turned back to Coby. "Very well. I am getting rather peckish." He removed his paw from Coby's chest, and the fur on his form rippled and melted away.

Four legs became two as his front paws turned into long pale hands with sharp nails on the ends of his fingers. The fur on his body shifted and settled onto his head where it fell into a waterfall of pale purple hair. He wore baggy pants and a wraparound shirt, leaving a long expansion of his chest exposed. A thick fur of purple and black just like his pelt had been hung over his shoulder, and his hand sat on it with a strange sort of tenderness.

"There, that's better." Cheshire flipped his hair over his shoulder, exposing his pointed ears decorated with gleaming diamond studs. He held a hand out to Coby which the twin took and helped him to his feet.

Coby took one look at my gaping face and snorted. "Show off."

Arching a brow in my direction, Cheshire stroked the long thickness of what I now realized was his tail as it hung over his shoulder, even if the movement of his hand suggested he was touching something else entirely. Fangs peaked from between his lips in a salacious smirk, telling me he knew

160

exactly what I was thinking. If anyone back home ever found out I was sexually attracted to a cat, they'd have me thrown in the asylum before you could say 'Tea Time!'

"I do not believe we have been properly introduced." Cheshire half-bowed to me, taking my hand. He brought it up to his mouth where, instead of kissing it like the others, he turned my palm over. His tongue darted out and licked my wrist, pulling a gasp from me at the action and the unexpected roughness of his tongue. Lifting his head slightly to give me a heated look, he purred. "I am Cheshire Cat. You may call me Cheshire or Cat, but never pussycat." He shot a warning glare at Coby who bit his knuckles to fight a smile.

A bit overwhelmed by the figure before me, I found myself at a loss for words. "I... um... I'm Ally. I mean, Alice." I gave a small curtsy. "At your service."

Cheshire straightened and gave me a once over. "Yes, you will be."

"What's going on?" Carban's voice called out, and we spun around to see his head peeking out of the surface of the tree trunk. "Are you going to stand out there and chit chat all day? We have things to do. A wedding to attend. And I like my head where it is." He didn't wait for our reply before his head disappeared back into the tree.

"That brother of yours needs to wet his dick so that maybe he might loosen that stick shoved so far up his ass." Cheshire and Coby laughed before the cat turned his eyes on me. "Maybe after we're done, you can help him with that?"

I gaped at the cat. My hand lifted, and I was one second away from smacking that arrogant smile on his face when Carban yelled for us again.

Cheshire turned away from me and waved us forward. "Come inside before someone else decides to bother me with a visit."

CHAPTER

STEPPING THROUGH THE SIDE of the tree wasn't like anything I expected it to be. It was far too easy and over just as quickly, as if stepping from one room and into another.

One moment I was outside of the willow, the gleaming vines hanging overhead, and the next, I was standing in the doorway of a nicely furnished living room. Carban lay spread out on a couch of cream-colored fabric, a golden chalice in his hand. He sipped from it with a lazy expression on his face.

"Sit." Cheshire waved an arm toward the chair. I moved to do as he asked but he stopped me with a single hand. "Not you. Him." He inclined his head at Coby who wagged his brows but did as he was bid.

"And what about me?" I asked, lifting my chin to stare the cat down. "Should I sit on the floor like a dog and wait for your call?"

Amusement rolled from the cat as he stroked his tail and then angled his head toward a door. "In there... unless you'd like an audience?"

My brows furrowed. Why would we need privacy for him to let us use his looking glass? My eyes moved from the cat to the twins who watched me with growing amusement. Well, Coby did. Carban seemed to be put off by the whole thing... or maybe that was just his normal face.

Since they weren't objecting, I walked toward the door, allowing the cat to open it for me before we stepped inside what appeared to be his bedroom. A large bed filled most of the room, covered in silken cream sheets and more pillows than I could count. Off to one side stood a closet with its door left open and clothing falling out onto the floor.

"Would you like to wash first?" Cheshire nodded toward another door across the room. "The bathroom is through there."

I eyeballed the door and then shook my head. "Uh, no. I'm alright. Thank you. I'd just like to get this over with. Where's the mir—" My words were cut off as I turned around to

164

see Cheshire had opened his shirt. "Why are you taking your clothes off?" I gaped at the beautiful man with the pointed ears and thick tail hanging over his shoulder.

His emerald green eyes rolled over to look at me with a disinterested expression. "Would you rather we mated with our clothes on?"

"Mate?" My voice raised to such an octave that Cheshire winced. "You mean as in... sex?"

Lips pursed, Cheshire lifted an elegant brow. "The queen sent you, correct?"

"Yes...?"

"Then what is the problem? Would you prefer me in cat form?" He lifted his hand, the fingernails so long they could be called claws. "Do not feel ashamed. Many do so enjoy it. I know I do." His hands dipped inside of his shirt, pushing the edges open and pulling it from his pants as he let it droop off his shoulders.

I flushed and gasped in a mixture of horror and attraction. Once I got over my initial surprise, the sheer audacity of the implications the cat dared to mutter in my direction should have sent me in a tailspin, but it only frustrated me.

Crossing my arms under my chest and staring him down, I asked, "What, by everything that is good, do you think the queen sent me for?"

Cheshire's eyes dipped down to my breasts where my corset and my arms had pushed them up to an almost obscene view. I dropped my arms and shifted away from him, turning to face the other direction. I couldn't look at him with his shirt off, the image of his lean muscular form too much of a distraction.

"It's alright to be nervous," he murmured, no more teasing in his voice. His footsteps were quiet on the soft carpet of the bedroom. Strong warm fingers curled over my shoulders, moving in soothing circles along my tense muscles. He kneaded the flesh, and my head lulled. A small whimper slipped out of my throat, and that made him chuckle. "See, this doesn't have to be a chore. The queen wishes us to mate, but we could be much more than that, if you were so inclined."

My eyes fluttered closed, my head rolling to the side as I barely registered his words. His mouth found the junction of my neck where his tongue lapped at my skin. A sharp sting made me hiss, and I jerked away from him, my hand clutching my neck.

"You bit me."

Cheshire's brows furrowed, his tongue flicking out to lick the blood from his lip. "What is that?" He ignored my outraged and brushed his fingers over his lips, his mouth smacking as he thought aloud, "What is that I taste?"

"If you don't like the taste of me, you can't blame me," I snapped, stomping to the bathroom. I shoved the door open and searched for something to clean and bandage my neck. Opening and shutting drawers, I didn't pay the cat much mind as he came marching in behind me.

"You're a human." He said it like it was something disgusting, as if I had offended him by being what I am.

"Of course, I am," I called over my shoulder, grabbing a rag from the drawer and wetting it in the sink. I winced as I touched it to the nick on my neck and turned to give the cat the full force of my glare. "What did you think I was doing here with the Tweedles? We're trying to get to the palace, not whore our way through the whole Underground."

Cheshire rubbed the sides of his forehead, his eyes going to the ceiling in a silent prayer. "Then why didn't you lead with that?"

"Well, you were a bit busy planning on who else I could fuck after you had your fill," I reminded him with a sneer. I shoved past him and back into the bedroom where I hurried through to the living area. The cloth still on my neck, I shouted at the twins. "Get up both of you. We're leaving."

Coby and Carban looked up from the game of cards they were playing on the couch. When their eyes landed on me and then the cloth, their eyes widened, and they jumped to their feet.

"What happened?" Coby came to my side, reaching for the cloth.

I moved away from his hands with a scowl. "You need better friends."

Carban didn't wait for me to give permission but snatched the cloth from my hand and jerked my head to the side. "Did he do this to you?"

"I already apologized," Cheshire announced from the bedroom door. Carban released me and came at Cheshire, grabbing the cat by the throat.

"No, you didn't," I argued, marching over to where he stood.

Carban squeezed his hand, making the cat flinch. "You hurt her."

"No, I tasted her as I would have done with anyone I meant to bed," Cheshire

168

growled, shoving Carban away from him. "I just didn't know that she wasn't for mating." His eyes moved to me, and his head dipped. "My apologies for the misunderstanding."

I studied him for a moment, my lips pressed into a tight line. "You are forgiven on the chance that you will allow us to use your looking glass to get to the Unseelie Palace."

Coby snickered. "She's got you by the tail now, Cheshire. Better give her what she wants lest she cry foul and the queen finds out."

Cheshire snarled at Coby and then jerked his head toward the wall where a long mirror hung. "It's there, but you shouldn't go out there bleeding like you are."

"Well then, bandage it, and we will be on our way." I dropped the cloth and arched a brow at him. "It's your fault after all."

Still shirtless, Cheshire slid his hands over his chest and cupped his tail, sliding his fingers through the fur with a pensive expression. "Yes, you are correct. However, I think we are uneven as we are now."

"Uneven?" I arched a brow and glanced at the twins. They shifted uncomfortably beneath my gaze and didn't offer up any help.

"Yes," Cheshire continued. "I have nicked you, yes. I have insulted you, agreed.

169

However, the use of my looking glass has a higher price than your honor."

"Excuse me," I cried out, my brows shooting up to my hairline and my mouth dropping opening. "I have to disagree. You very nearly took the one thing I haven't messed up in my life by accident, and you think it's not worth the same as your ridiculous magic mirror?" I waved a hand carelessly at the object on the wall.

"So, you are a virgin." Cheshire smiled broadly, licking his lips. "I thought you might be. You blush far too much for a seasoned woman. I only have my shirt off, and you can't keep your eyes off me."

"Yes, I can," I snapped and then caught my eyes dipping down to follow his hands across his pecs and down his abdomen. "I mean... stop distracting me and put on your clothes. What is wrong with you people? Don't you have a sense of decorum?" I moved my weight from one foot to the other, shaking my head. "I've never met a group of people so against clothing. I like being naked as much as the next person, but this is ridiculous."

Coby patted me on the shoulder. "It's alright, Ally dear. You don't have to do anything you don't want to do, but you really should let Cheshire close the wound. He can at least do that right."

170

I eyed him warily for a moment and then nodded, resigning to let the cat fix me. Sitting down on a nearby chair, I splayed my skirts out around me and smoothed them over my legs. "Very well. Let's get on with it. Hatter will be here shortly, and I don't want to have to explain this to him."

"What does that mad old man have to do with anything?" Cheshire mused, kneeling beside me.

"Oh, didn't we tell you?" Coby said in a sing-song voice, earning him a warning look from me. "They're engaged to be engaged. Well, as soon as she tells her human that she's leaving him."

Cheshire arched a perfectly shaped brow at me, brushing my hair away from my neck. "Not whoring yourself through the Underground, hmmm?"

I was tempted to stick my tongue out at him but settled for a scathing glower, turning my face from him. "Just get on with it already."

Carban chuckled and sneered, "Words he's never had directed toward him."

"As if I have any control over how others perceive me. I cannot help that I am irresistible." Cheshire flashed his fangs at me.

"And humble too," I countered, making him frown.

"More of a curse than a blessing," he murmured to himself more than anything. "Now, I'm not going to hurt you, so control your urge to hit me."

"Fine," I huffed, placing my hands in my lap and forcing myself to stay still. "I will try to keep my hands to myself."

"Much appreciated."

I waited for the cat to do some kind of magic to close my wound, but there were no preparations, no sparkles or flash of lights. Then Cheshire leaned forward and pressed his mouth to my neck once more.

I tensed, my hand itching to push him away.

"Relax," he purred against my neck. "I won't bite you again. Not unless you beg for it."

Rolling my eyes, I sighed. "Never."

A rumbling laugh reached me in return. "Never is an awfully long time." Then his wet rough tongue found the edges of my bite. It rolled and licked across the torn flesh, causing warmth to spread through my body. I shifted in my seat, suddenly finding an uncomfortable ache between my thighs. The hands that itched to push him away wanted to pull him closer.

My face turned toward him, my nose burying into his hair. He smelled of vanilla and cherry blossoms. The scent made my pulse race and my mouth water. Before I could think less of it, my hands moved from my lap and latched onto his pants, pulling him closer to me.

"There you go, love," Cheshire murmured against my skin, making no move to leave me. "All healed."

Not caring about my wound any longer, I laced my fingers into his hair and jerked his mouth to mine. The twins made a sound, a mixture of amusement and disapproval that I noted for later as my mouth and mind were otherwise preoccupied with the Fae before me.

"I see you have even charmed the notoriously horrid cat, my dear Alice," Hatter commented from somewhere in the willow, and I jerked my mouth away from Cheshire's blushing furiously. "I wouldn't expect anything less."

CHAPTER

15

NOTHING COOLS A ROOM faster than when
your new kind-of fiancé enters the room
while you are sort-of kissing another man
you just met twenty minutes ago. However,
as far as fiancés went, Hatter did an excellent
job keeping his head about it.

Jumping out of my seat, I shoved
Cheshire out of the way and rushed to
Hatter's side. "This isn't what it looks like."

Mercury chuckled, his eyes twinkling
with mirth. Wrapping his arms around me,
he drew me up to him, pecking my nose. "You
have nothing to fear from me, Alice dear. As
I told you, any of your love is fine by me. You
won't lose me just because you find yourself
caring for others, especially if those others
are just as charming as you are. I'd be
surprised if you could resist any of them."

174

My mouth drooped open, and my body warmed at his words. Once more, Mercury has taught me that my expectations for a husband had been so low that I didn't know what I'd been missing. Even if I went back and somehow Lewis convinced me he wasn't a lying bastard, I wouldn't be able to forget Mercury's loving adoration and, not to forget, talented mouth.

"Mercury," Cheshire purred, moving off of the ground where I'd left him and prowling over to our side, "so good to see you. I didn't know you'd be stopping by today. I'd have dressed down."

His crystalline eyes scanned up and down Hatter's form, the hunger in his gaze even more eager than it had been to have me out of my dress. My shocked expression went to the twins who just seemed bored by the whole situation now.

"Cheshire." Hatter released me partly to shift sideways, his arm reached out, and then next thing I knew, my eyes are bugging out of my head. Hatter had his hand on the back of Cheshire's head and his mouth angled over the cat's. I was so close to them that I could see their tongue brushing against one another, and I couldn't find a reason to stop them.

175

"You two are going to give Ally a heart attack." Coby chuckled, taking me from Hatter's arms. He waved a hand in front of my face which I appreciated because I was feeling a bit overheated. I'd hate to faint and miss any of this.

Cheshire released Hatter and purred, sliding his tongue along his lips. "My apologies, I forgot you were here."

Carban snorted. "Sure, you did. Can we leave already? The queen will not be patient for long. The fact that we haven't had a single message telling us to hurry up is a fucking miracle. Let's all do ourselves a favor and keep our heads."

I pushed Coby away from me and waved my hands. "I agree with Carban. We have gotten completely off topic." I pointed a finger between the two of them. "How long have you two been together? And when were you going tell me about him during your whole 'I'm happy just to have some of your love' speech."

Hatter beamed at me, tipping his hat. "And I meant it. Do you not feel the same? Would it make you happier if I only kissed you? Only whispered sweet nothings in your ears?" He took my hand, pulling me closer to him. "I wasn't aware you needed such a commitment, but I would be more than happy to oblige."

Cheshire harrumphed and slinked away from us. "Well, I will just go put my shirt back on since no one here wants me." He threw his tail back over his shoulder, stroking his hand up and down it as if comforting himself.

"Now, now, Cheshire, no need to pout." Hatter winked at the cat, still holding me close. "It's not like you don't have other lovers. Aren't you waiting for someone from the queen?"

"That reminds me!" I smacked Hatter on the chest, and hissed in his ear. "Don't you have something that belongs to me?" Without his permission, I reached into his pocket and grabbed my drawers before excusing myself to Cheshire's room.

I took a moment to gather my thoughts while I put my drawers back on. Hatter was alright with me being with other men, but he also wanted to be with other men as well. Did that mean he wanted to see other women? How exactly did that work if we were to marry? I knew in the human realm there were whispers of people having relations with those of the same gender, but I'd never expected to see it right in front of me, let alone have it affect me so much.

I adjusted my clothing while I tried to calm myself down. This whole adventure has been one new experience after another. If I ever made it back home, I'd have so much to tell Rhoda. She would have a fit if she knew what I knew.

A knock sounded on the door before Coby opened it. "Are you alright, Ally?"

Sighing, I tucked a hair behind my ears and nodded. "I'm fine. A bit overwhelmed by it all." I pressed my hands to my stomach, smoothing my hands down my dress. "This is all a bit new to me. I'm not sure exactly how I should be feeling."

"That's perfectly natural," Coby told me, moving further into the room. He didn't approach me thankfully, giving me my space as he sat on the edge of Cheshire's bed. "I can imagine you don't have many problems like this in your realm. From what I remember of the human realm they are a bit prudish and judgmental, except for your ancient Greeks," Coby tilted his head to the side and grinned, "and those Romans sure knew how to throw a party."

My brow furrowed. "How old are you?"

"I just had my three thousandth birthday." At my surprised expression, Coby cleared his throat and adjusted his vest. "I'll have you know that I'm young for my age.

Fae live a long time. Our sense of time is quite different from yours. Time passes differently as we've told you before."

"Oh, my." I pressed a hand to my chest and shook my head. "Of course, it all makes sense now. No wonder Mercury didn't see a problem with me being with you or him being with Cheshire. You all live forever, and I'll..." I trailed off, suddenly feeling depressed. "I'll die long before I even make any kind of impression on any of your lives."

"Now, that's just not true," Hatter argued, pushing the door open and coming to my side. Cheshire followed him as well but only to get his shirt, which he then took back into the other room where I assumed Carban waited.

"It's not?"

"Of course not, Alice dear." Hatter took both of my hands in his and brought them to his mouth. "I've waited centuries for someone to warm my heart the way you do mine. I'd never do anything that would hurt you, including being with anyone else. When I promised that I'd take care of you, I meant it. Until my dying day."

I let out a bitter laugh. "Mine will come before yours so that will be a short promise." Before Hatter could argue, I pressed a hand to his mouth. "Forget it. Let's just enjoy us while it lasts. I'm not asking you to give up Cheshire because quite frankly I wouldn't want to give up someone who could kiss the way he did either. But while I'm alright with the men, I'm not sure I'd be comfortable sharing you with other women." I shifted in place, wrapping my arms around my waist.

"Then you have nothing to fear." Hatter beamed. "I haven't loved a woman in four thousand years until you."

I feared to ask him how old he actually was. If Coby and Carban were three thousand and were considered young, how old exactly was the rest of them? I was barely twenty and thought I was getting old. My mother would have a heart attack within two minutes of coming to this world.

Tired of the whole conversation, I wrapped my arms around him and held him tight. "Thank you. I think we should get moving now."

"Fucking finally!" Carban shouted from the other room.

We moved out of the bedroom and gathered around the mirror. Cheshire had put his shirt back on, but I couldn't figure out if I were happy or disappointed by that. All these men so interested in me was making my hormones confused. It didn't know what to do. Perhaps this was why they didn't want us to think about our marital bed until after we were married. Once you had a taste, you never wanted to stop.

I knew I didn't.

"What are you thinking about, Alice dear?" Hatter murmured in my ear, his hands resting on my hips while we waited for Cheshire to activate his mirror. "Your scent has spiked, and I'm not sure I'll be able to wait much longer to have another taste of you if you keep smelling the way you do."

"A little less noise from the peanut gallery." Carban shot us a warning look before gesturing to Cheshire. "Does this thing work or not? Why is it taking so long?"

"You're talking an awful lot lately," I mused, eyeballing the twin. "Need to hit your word count before the end of the day?"

Giving me the evil eye, Carban sniffed. "Impatient to be done with it. If I have to watch one more of these imbeciles paw at you, I'll fall on my own scissors."

"Keep your pins in your pocket," Cheshire growled as he trailed a hand over the frame. "I'm almost done."

As the surface of the mirror rippled and swirled, Coby snickered. "I think my brother is maybe a bit jealous."

I eyed Carban for any hint that what Coby said was true, but the twin had a blank facial expression... which might have been a clue. However, I didn't have time to think too much about it because the portal was ready.

"There we go. All set. You're welcome." Cheshire flicked his hair and studied his nails. What? Did he expect some kind of big reaction?

"Thank Reaper." Carban didn't wait for any of us before practically throwing himself through the mirror frame.

Shaking his head, Coby ran a hand through his hair. "Couldn't get out of here fast enough. The poor man. In any case, we'll meet in the garden." He brushed his fingertips along my jawline and then tapped my nose. "I'll hold my breath until you arrive."

My lips pulled at the edges, my cheeks aching from the effort. "Don't die on my account."

Cheshire waited to enter last with Hatter and me. I released Hatter and approached the mirror. Poking a finger into the liquid, I asked, "How exactly does this work?"

"Magic, of course." Cheshire yawned and placed a hand on the side of his face. "You just walk into it while thinking of where you want to go. Then the magic takes you there. It only works for certain Fae."

"So, we couldn't have used it without your help?"

Cheshire gave me a lazy grin. "Yes, and keep in mind that you still owe me for this. I plan to collect."

Flushing at the heated look he gave me, I turned to Hatter. "Should we go together?"

Hatter shook his head. "No, if we go together, we take the chance of coming back out the other side all wrong." He waved a hand down my form. "I prefer you the way you are, though you could do with fewer layers."

I giggled and pushed at his chest. "Stop it. I'll go first then you can follow me."

"I'm happy to follow you anywhere, Alice dear." He pressed his lips to the corner of my mouth before releasing me. I took a deep breath and walked into the mirror's frame.

CHAPTER

THE COOL LIQUID GLASS covered me, and for a moment, I forgot I was supposed to be thinking of where I wanted to go. It didn't make much sense to me. The other mirror didn't require my participation, but who was I to question the magic of the Underground?

When I stepped out of the mirror and into a large dark-colored bedroom alone, I had a feeling something had gone terribly wrong. The men were nowhere to be seen and the room too dark. The shadows too large. My skin prickled with an unknown fear.

Someone was watching me.

Turning around the room, I searched for that unknown. My heart raced as the shadows began to move. Despite myself, my eyes locked onto them, watching them writhe and whisper. Then they jumped at me, and everything went dark.

When I opened my eyes again, I thought I was dreaming. However, if I was indeed dreaming, it was not like any dream I'd ever experienced. The dark shadowy room had dissipated, and in its place, a watercolor world spread out around me.

I was back in the Tundrey Woods, amidst another Tea Party. Except Twinkle, Hare, and the Doormouse had been replaced with the twins and Cheshire. They talked amongst themselves, seemingly not noticing me there. It was like having water in your ears. I could hear them but not enough to actually make out what they were saying.

Moving around the table, I watched them. Each of them attractive to me in their own way. Each of them with their own personalities and aspects about them I cared for. Even Cheshire who I'd only just met pulled at something in my heart.

"You can't stay."

"What?" I spun around and stared at Hatter. "Why not?"

Hatter didn't meet my gaze as he lifted his teacup to his lips and sipped from it. He was speaking to me but not. It was quite the conundrum, and just when I thought he wouldn't say anything else, his eyes locked

185

with mine. Those big stormy gray eyes that held such love and adoration now were hard as stone.

"You're a human. You don't belong here. Go back to your world and leave us to it."

I gaped at him, backing away from the table with tears in my eyes. I knew I didn't belong, that my time with them was limited, but to hear Hatter say those words made them even more real.

"We can help you." The combined words of many burned my ears, jerking my eyes away from the table. My head whipped from side to side as I searched for the owners of the voice, my attention no longer on the men I'd come to care for here in the Underground.

"Help me do what?" I asked the stranger, my own voice coming out odd.

At first, the creature didn't answer, and then I saw it. The thing I'd seen in the bedroom just moments before.

The shadows.

Like something living inside the inky blackness, it moved and shifted until it formed one single figure. It didn't step out of the dark, and I knew in my gut that I had to stay away. Touching them would not end well for me.

"Stay," the shadowy figure hiding in between the trees hissed at me. "That is what you want, is it not, Alice Liddell?"

I didn't like the sound of my name on their lips. I didn't like how they resounded deep inside of me, making me feel things I wouldn't otherwise feel. Their words tugged on a desire in me, the desperation to stay with the others and turn from my human world.

Pushing the feeling down, I took a step forward. "How do you know my name?"

"You should be more careful with what you say in the dark." A dark collective chuckle made my insides twist unpleasantly. "Even we have ears."

Ignoring its cryptic words, I moved around Hatter's table and closer to the figure. "You know my name. It's only fair that I know yours... and what do you want in return for helping me?"

I glanced back at the table where they went about drinking their tea as if I weren't there. No matter our issues I could not bear the thought of going back to my world and never seeing them again. If I could stay with them even for a bit longer, I would.

I could hear the figure slithering around behind me, a malevolent presence that caused a chill in my blood.

"Why, dear Alice, you may call us the Shadows, for that is all we are now, and all we ask is for one simple favor."

"Simple it may be to you, but as you know, I am a human. I cannot do magic. I'm not strong. I have nothing to offer you," I reminded them, placing my hands on my hips and nodding just so. "What could I possibly have to offer you in return?"

The shadows chortled.

"It's not a laughing matter. Either tell me what you want or let me go. I only have a short time left in the Underground, and I do not fancy wasting them with you." I hated the helpless feeling inside my stomach. I'd have to go back to my world. Face those that I have left with questions unanswered. Lewis. My mother. Even my siblings. They would all want answers, answers that would surely put me in the loony bin.

"So impatient, little human, but we suppose you are right. Time grows short." The shadows shifted from behind one tree until they were near another, much closer to me this time. I forced myself not to step back.

Grow a spine, Alice.

"State your business." I crossed my arms over my chest and lifted my chin, hoping to put off an air of confidence when my knees were shaking.

Letting out a small chuckle, the shadows hissed, "Do you know of the Seelie Princess?"

I frowned. "Yes, what of her?"

"Our dear prince and princess are having a hard time. They cannot admit their own feelings," the shadows began, making my brow furrow in confusion. "A wedding without love is no wedding at all. Don't you agree?"

"So, what is to be done about it?" I countered. "I don't know them well enough to mess with their affairs, let alone know what to do to make them admit their feelings."

"Ah, but you are wrong, Ms. Liddell. You will have every chance to help them when you become Fae."

The shadows were quiet as I gaped at them. "What do you mean when you say that become Fae? One cannot simply change what they are, can they?"

"Of course, they can. You can." The shadows moved around another tree, seemingly teasing me with its presence as I became anxious to hear their words.

"How?"

"There is an Orchard," they started, their tone bored, "not far from the palace. In that Orchard lies a door. You have a key to that door." My hand went to my pocket, instinctively patting the key there. "The door will take you home, or…" The smile in their voice made my stomach twist into knots.

When they didn't finish right away, I stepped closer to them. "Or?"

"Or you could look to the left and find something even better." The shadows paused and whispered amongst themselves, too low for me to catch the words. "Find the tree that hides from us. It will give you what you want, and when you have become Fae, when you are finally able to stay here with your loved ones, then you will do as we ask."

"But I don't know what it is you even want!" I shouted back at the shadows, my fingers curled into fists until my nails bit into my hands, making me wince. If I were dreaming, it shouldn't hurt, should it? I almost laughed at the thought. Didn't I have that exact same one after entering Wonderland?

"A word of caution, Alice Liddell," the shadows growled, not answering my question. "Do not think to betray us. We are not the Fae of your dreams but of your nightmares. If you do not hold up your end of the deal, we will find you, and we will end you."

Before I could answer in return, the scene began to melt away. The shadows closed in around me, and then I was bolting up from where I laid on the ground of the bedroom I'd been in before.

The sound of a door opening pulled my attention away from the surprisingly brighter bedroom. Hatter stood in the doorway, a mixture of concern and relief on his face.

"Oh, Alice dear, there you are." Hatter rushed to my side and helped me stand to my feet. "When you didn't come through the mirror with us, we were worried sick."

Coby waited by the door as we walked over to it. "How in the Underground did you end up in the queen's bedroom, Ally?"

I shook my head, not giving away what had happened. "I don't know. One minute I was in Cheshire's house, and then the next, I'm here."

"Well, let's get you down to the party. You're missing quite a bit of fun." Hatter grinned, pressing his lips to the side of my head.

Nodding, I leaned into his embrace as my eyes trailed back to the room I'd been in and the offer the shadows had given me. Whatever was I going to do?

CHAPTER

IV

COBY AND HATTER LED me through the palace and down into a gorgeous garden. This one was much different than the Seelie Queen's. Roses decorated every inch of the place with other kinds of flowers blended in to match.

In the center of the garden stood a large tree, a man and woman embraced beneath the tree while a third woman watched them before behind it. I had a moment to wonder about the significance to the portrayal before we approached a table full of food.

The others were already at the table, eating their fill. Cheshire lounged lazily on a chair, licking frosting from a spoon in an obscene manner which drew the eyes of many of the table's occupants. When he saw me looking, his lips pulled at the edges, and he dipped the whole spoon into his mouth and pulled it out slowly, never losing eye contact with me.

My body warmed, and for a second, I forgot about what had just happened to me. "This looks lovely." I took the seat Hatter held open for me next to Carban who spun a knife around on the top of the table.

"Where did you find her?" He glanced up from his plate to look me over as if making sure I was really there and safe.

"In the Queen's room," Coby answered, popping a grape into his mouth as he plopped down in a chair across from his brother and next to Cheshire.

"I see, I was right," a smooth and sultry voice answered as a tall, pale woman clothed in black came around a green hedge, the prince at her side. "I thought I felt someone come through my mirror." Her dark blue eyes landed on me, and she gave a knowing smile. "I am glad to see you are all right, Alice Liddell."

I stared at the woman for a moment. I knew her. I felt it nagging at the back of my head. Blood red lips and long nails, silky black hair that fell around her shoulders like a waterfall. If I didn't know any better, I'd say she and the prince were siblings, but the way the others stiffened at her presence and some even bowed told me differently.

The prince kissed his mother on the cheek and took his place at the table. "Mother, please. We don't have long before they arrive. You can play your games later."

The dark queen moved around the table as if she were gliding through the air. The long sleeves of her black gown draped over her hands and made her seem as if she might be a specter rather than the Unseelie Queen.

"Thank you, Your Majesty." Hatter knelt at her side, taking her hand between his own as she sat in her chair. "I am forever grateful to find my Alice."

"Of course, you are." The queen smiled not at Hatter, but at me, like she knew I had been doing something naughty in her room, but she wouldn't tell. Arching a dark brow, she mused, "Let's not lose her again, shall we?"

"Never." Hatter tipped his hat and stood before taking his place by my side. He filled my plate with different foods, some I recognized while others I didn't, but I wasn't hungry. I should be after all the time I'd been there, but all I could think about was the shadows and their offer.

What was I going to do? The shadows had practically given me my dream on a silver platter.

If I did as they said, it would solve everything. I wouldn't have to go back to the human world and marry Lewis. I could stay here with Hatter and the others. Also, from the way the shadows had implied it, I would have magic as well, so no more being the victim. No more being the weakest of them.

I could finally take care of them.

"What's in your head?" Hatter asked, tapping my forehead with a finger.

I shook my head and offered him a small smile. "Nothing. Just savoring this moment." I placed my hand on his and squeezed it. "I never want to forget it."

"And you won't," Carban said from my other side. "You may have to go back, but you will visit, won't you?"

"I- I want to, but the seer..." I drew out, not sure how to explain what he had said any better than what I'd heard. "I'm not sure if I can come back."

"Nonsense." Coby waved his fork at me. "That old coot isn't all-knowing. You can't take everything he says as gospel."

"Quite right," the prince agreed, his eyes locking onto his mother. I had a feeling they weren't talking about the same thing as us.

The prince then angled his head toward me. "Alice, do you remember how to get home? I know you were having issues remembering."

"Um. I think so. It's in the Orchard, correct?"

I avoided the curious look Cheshire gave me, one that said he thought there was something I wasn't telling. Did I smell like I was lying? I didn't have the same kind of senses as them. I couldn't smell the difference between one emotion to another. Keeping their individual smells separate was hard enough.

"If you're done eating, I can show you where it is," the prince offered, taking a drink from his own glass. "My princess will be here soon, and we won't have time after that to get away."

"Oh, Your Highness, you don't have to do that," Hatter insisted. "I can show her. Why don't you enjoy your meal?"

"Nonsense." The prince shook his head, his long red earring swaying from side to side. "You rest. When the princess gets here, she'll be needing you and the Tweedles to get her things sorted. Let me play tour guide for once. I may not get another chance." He gave me a grin and a wink.

"Yes, the life of a married man is quite droll." Cheshire rolled his head in the prince's direction. "I suppose I will be slotted for one before long if the other one gets her way."

"My cousin is quite insistent," the dark queen murmured, looking up from beneath her lashes. They were talking about things I didn't know, things I had been meaning to ask about but hadn't had the chance.

I glanced back to Cheshire and opened my mouth, but he licked his thumb and stopped me. "Not now, love. Later."

Sighing, I leaned back in my chair. I picked at my food, taking a few bites, but then sat my fork down. I couldn't eat. Not now.

"Are you ready?" The prince appeared at my shoulder, holding a hand out to me.

Nodding, I placed my napkin on the table and then stood. Hatter's arm shot out and pulled me to him. His mouth brushed along the seam of mine, and he held me tight. "Don't tarry long, Alice dear. I wish to make you remember me for a lifetime."

My toes curled at his words, and I grinned up at him before taking the prince's hand and leaving the table.

We moved through the hedges at the back of the garden, a maze on its own that I would have had difficulty maneuvering by myself. I held tight to the prince's hand, not wanting to get lost like I'd done in the woods.

"Do you love the princess?" I asked out of nowhere. I hadn't even been thinking about what the shadows had said, but apparently, I hadn't forgotten about it.

The prince frowned at me. "Of course, I do. Why would you think otherwise?"

I lifted a shoulder and dropped it. "Just wondering. I wasn't sure if your marriage was one of convenience like what waited for me at home."

Before the prince could answer, we exited the hedge maze and stood at the entrance to a large Orchard. Rows and rows of trees stood tall and silent, waiting to be harvested. I didn't see the door or the tree that the shadows had spoken of though.

"Where is it?" I asked, turning to the prince.

"Where's what?" The prince arched his brows turning from the view.

"The door, the one the key goes to." I reached into my pocket and pulled out the key I had stolen from Type and Gripe.

The prince clucked his tongue. "You shouldn't have taken that. Those two bird heads are going to have a fit."

"How else was I going to get in then? The door was locked."

Sighing and flipping his hair over his shoulder, the prince started down the small hill before us. "There is a reason for that, a warning you should have heeded."

I followed him, trying to keep pace with his long legs. "The shadows, you mean?"

"Yes," he murmured. "I fear this world will be at war before long, and that is no place for a human. You are better off going home and staying there."

I gaped at him. "I can't. I can't just leave."

Pausing in mid-step, the prince turned to me and pursed his lips. "I suppose not. You have quite the group of admirers. I've never seen the cat so enamored by someone before, not to mention the Tweedles." He shook his head. "Those two will fuck anything that walks, and most would willingly do so, but you seem to be immune to their advances." He chuckled at my shocked expression. "Do not look so surprised. That is probably what appeals to them so much."

We walked for a few more moments before we stopped before a door. This door, much like all the others I'd come across, seemed out of place along the wall that surrounded the Orchard. The key in my pocket warmed against my thigh as if knowing I would need to use it.

My eyes searched for the tree the shadows had told me would grant me my wish but didn't see it. I didn't want to ask the prince in case he got suspicious. I'd have to come back to find it later after everyone went to sleep.

"What do you say? Shall we head back?" the prince asked, glancing around the Orchard. He seemed anxious to get moving.

"Hoping your princess has arrived?" I teased, poking him on the arm.

The prince beamed down at me. "I am that easy to read, am I?"

I threw my head back and laughed. "No easier than if your heart were sown onto your sleeve." I placed a hand on his arm and squeezed. "No worries, I know how you feel. I—" My eyes caught sight of a beautiful white head of hair coming our way.

The prince turned from me, and the expression of pure admiration told me this was his bride to be, the Seelie princess and the daughter of the icy queen who'd threatened our lives. Was she like her mother, or had this one taken after her father?

"My peach," the prince's voice dropped an octave, and he moved from me to embrace the woman. They held each other so tightly that I thought maybe they had forgotten I was even there, but then the woman's eyes peeked out from his shoulder to zero in on me.

She did not like me. Not one bit.

Instead of commenting, she turned back to her prince. "Hello." She held him tight, joy in her eyes. "I couldn't find you at the palace. Your mother brought me here."

I didn't know what the shadows were talking about. The two of them clearly loved each other. There's nothing I could do here to make them love each other more than they did. So what if they haven't said the words?

"Of course, she would." The prince pulled back from the hug and brushed the princess's hair behind her ear with such tenderness that I felt like I was an interloper on their private moment. The prince continued to speak to her as if I weren't there. "I am happy you arrived safely. I meant to be there when you arrived, but something came up."

"Something?" The princess's eyes shot to me, and I shifted in place.

The prince gestured toward me and urged me to come to meet his princess. I was hesitant to do as he bid but didn't want to be rude. Moving closer to him, I tried to keep my distance so as not to make the princess feel even more threatened by me.

"This is Ms. Liddell. She is visiting from the human world."

I dipped down in a curtsy, amused by the two of them. For two people who claimed to love one another, they were awfully stiff now that I was near. The princess clearly saw me as something to fear, and that, at least, meant she cared for the prince. Maybe I wouldn't have to do much to get these two to admit their feelings for one another.

"It's a pleasure to meet the one who has captured our dark prince's heart." I beamed at her, laughter coloring my voice as she blushed at my words. This one was even worse than me. If any of the two weren't voicing their feelings, it had to be her.

"That's enough out of you." The prince scowled at me and waved an arm. "The Hatter is no doubt waiting for you."

I huffed and stomped a foot, annoyed that he would dismiss me so easily. "Fine, but don't blame me when you mess it all up." I marched away, leaving the two royals to hash out their own issues. I just hoped it was enough to pay the shadows back.

CHAPTER

THE PRINCE DIDN'T COME back with his princess until just after sunset. They had their heads down together and were whispering, smiles on their faces.

"Ally?" Coby pressed his thumbs harder into the heel of my foot drawing my attention back to him. "I'm feeling a bit neglected. Here I am rubbing your poor feet, and you only have eyes for the prince." Coby dipped his head and pouted, his dark hair falling over his eyes.

Shifting my weight on the blanket they'd set out for us in the garden to rest on, I gave Coby my full attention. "I'm sorry, I promise. No more distractions. I'm all yours."

"Only his?" Carban asked, surprising me.

He had his back half to us, eating on some fruit left over from dinner. It had been his idea to take the leftovers and a bottle of wine to sleep beneath the stars, a curiously thoughtful suggestion on his part.

I reached my hand out and placed it on his back. His eyes were down as he shifted toward me, almost afraid to look me in the eye. "You know what I mean."

"Do I?"

I removed my foot from Coby's hand and scooched closer to the other twin until my front pressed against his side, my head on his shoulder. "What do you want me to say, Carban? No games."

Carban didn't even hesitate before he locked eyes with me. "I don't want words. I want you."

The amount of need in his voice seeped into me, making my blood race in response. Licking my lips, I leaned my head back so that our noses brushed. "And what will you do with me once you have me? Will you push me away the moment you think I'm being influenced by your Fae magic like before?"

I took a large breath, inhaling his scent. Things low inside of me tightened and moistened ready for something I had yet to have.

"Just sitting here like this with you," I panted, my mouth dry and wanting, "makes my skin tight and the need to take my clothing off almost insufferable. Would you deny me?"

Carban opened his mouth to answer, but Cheshire interrupted, "For the love of my sanity, please think before you speak. Her arousal already tinges the air, and I do not think it is fair to the rest of us if you cast her aside. Think of your brother! Would you deny him the pleasure of her love simply because you fear she might not be completely in control of her desire?"

"It's not right," Carban muttered but didn't push me away. "We do not play fair."

"And how is that our fault?" Hatter sat up from where he lay curled around Cheshire. "We were born with it. Should we punish ourselves and the one we love because we cannot control it? She has not run screaming into the night the entire time our dear Alice has been with us. I would think that would be answer enough, don't you?" He arched a brow and picked up his hat where he had discarded it, placing it back on his head before laying back down on Cheshire's tail.

Coby, who had been quiet until now, watched his brother with a knowing intensity. "Ally has to leave soon. You and I know she might not be able to come back. Do not regret today for the sake of tomorrow."

The reminder of my limited lifespan here only made me more eager to know what I didn't before. If I went home and never came back, I'd regret not knowing what they tasted like. What it felt like to be at the mercy of their love. Lewis sure wouldn't be providing it.

"Please," I begged, curling my fingers into Carban's vest to pull him closer. "Kiss me."

The Tweedle seemed to think about it, and when he moved, I almost thought he was going to leave me again, but he only shifted so he could face me. His hands found the sides of my face, and he dragged me close, pulling me into his lap.

I straddled him, holding onto his vest as if my life depended on it, and in this moment, it felt like it. His mouth clashed with mine, and something inside of me broke. Desperation filled me, and I didn't care where we were or who watched. I needed him. I needed them all. Right now.

My fingers found the edges of his vest and pulled it away, shoving it down his arms and to the ground. Someone came up behind me and unlaced the corset of my dress. I released Carban long enough to let them take the contraption off me, and then their hands were cupping my breasts, kneading them until the peaks ached.

Gasping, I released Carban's mouth, and my head fell back, landing on Coby's shoulder. Peering up at him as his hands molded my breasts through my dress and his brother's hips rolled against my core, I felt truly trapped. I loved every moment of it.

Carban's lips found my neck, while his brother captured my mouth. My arms reached around and held onto Coby's neck, pulling him closer to me. One of them found the edge of my skirt and pushed it up, their fingers dipping between my thighs to caress my heat.

With a moan, I broke free of Coby's mouth. I had a moment to see Hatter move closer to us before my eyes fluttered shut in the wake of the onslaught of their ministrations. The sleeves of my dress were pushed down, and there was a rip. For a moment, I thought they had destroyed my dress, but then the fingers between my thighs plunged inside of me, causing me to cry out.

"That's it, Alice dear," Hatter murmured along my skin as he pulled the fabric away from my breasts and bared me to the garden. "Let us hear you," he urged me to call out as I rode the hand, Coby's hand, driving in and out of me.

The cool air pebbled my nipples, and I had a moment to wonder who was watching us. My eyes snapped open, and I searched the garden, but the sun had set, and only small lights from the bushes lit the area, leaving us in the shadows.

"Relax, love," Cheshire purred from where he had moved closer to watch us. "The only one watching you is me."

I let out a small laugh. "Is that supposed to make me feel better?" Carban's hand, I think, flicked a sensitive place between my thighs, and I gasped, my eyes darting to his amused face. "I'm going to die from pleasure, and I haven't even bedded any of you yet."

The men let out a collective chuckle dark and seductive, it rolled across my sensitive flesh and making me ache for more.

"Well, let us remedy that, shall we?" Hatter shot a look to Carban before reaching between us and undoing the laces of Carban's pants. He released the twin's length and gave it a small stroke and then a squeeze, making the quiet Fae moan.

I'd seen some of my sister Rhoda's anatomy books. I knew what a penis looked like, at least, in theory, but the sight of Carban hard and ready for me was a whole different experience. One that I didn't have a

208

chance to savor long before Coby was removing his hand and lifting me.

Carban leaned back on his elbows and allowed Hatter to position him at my center. My heart beat ratcheted up to twenty and panic set in. I forgot to breathe, my fingers digging into whoever's arm I could get a hold of, which happened to be Hatter's. He gave me a reassuring smile, rubbing Carban against me.

"Shh, it's alright. Breathe, Alice dear. Don't pass out on us now."

I nodded and did as he asked, bracing myself for what I'd been told would hurt. But instead of getting on with it, Hatter teased Carban and I, not giving either of us what we wanted until Carban croaked out, "No more, please. I'm not going to last."

With those words, Hatter inclined his head, and Coby lowered me onto his brother's length. It didn't hurt like I thought it would. A bit of pressure and a slight burning sensation, but that was soon forgotten when Coby urged me to move my hips.

Hatter's hand didn't leave my core as I rocked back and forth, his finger taking the place of Carban's, making sure I was good and truly consumed by the whole pleasure of it. My head lulled against Coby's shoulder as he helped me ride his brother, and my eyes peeked open to land on Cheshire where he stroked his tail in time with my movements. His eyes roamed over my bare form and where Carban and I connected. It didn't even bother me. In fact, it only made me move faster, wanting the cat to feel what I was feeling.

A low grunt came from Carban, and I was shifted off him. Carban moved over to Cheshire's side, and I was placed on my hands and knees. The junction between my thighs ached and throbbed but not in a completely unpleasant way. I certainly didn't protest when Coby slid inside of me from behind.

He lasted a lot longer than his brother, and before I knew it, I was crying out, my head falling between my arms. Hatter did not join in this time but sat to the side of us, his eyes on me as Coby mounted me like an animal. If my mother ever heard of this, I would not only be shunned but called a harlot. No woman in their right mind ever had relations except on their back and certainly not the way we had been doing it.

Hatter brushed my hair away from my face, our eyes locked together as my release hit me again. This time Coby grunted and slowed behind me, and I assumed he had finished as well.

Collapsing onto the blanket, I groaned. "No more." I shook my head and gave a small helpless whimper. "I can't take any more."

"Are you sure?" Hatter cooed, sliding his fingers down my spine before dipping them between my legs. "Cheshire might be happy to just watch, but I had so hoped to have you before you leave."

I rolled over onto my back and stared up at the beautiful man. His long silver hair hung around me like a curtain, his lips curled into a desire-ridden grin, almost manic at this point. At some point he had discarded his shirt and jacket, leaving him only in his pants and suspenders. The sight of him was truly something to behold.

Without a word, I spread myself for him, my arms reaching upward. We didn't rut like with the twins, racing to see who could finish first. Each movement was slow and calculating, Hatter would move inside of me for a moment and then shift his hips and have me gasping and writhing on the ground. By the time I hit my release, there were stars in my eyes. My back arched, and my mouth dropped open in a silent cry for more.

Hatter patted my hip and placed a kiss over my heart before helping me dress.

Cheshire crawled across the lawn, his eyes hooded with desire. "Let me help you clean up, love."

Too spent to argue with him, I stayed on my back until his rough tongue found the sensitive skin between my thighs. I cried out and moaned as he lapped at me, not trying to take me like the others but gently taking his time. By the time he sat up, licking his lips and stroking his tail, I couldn't move.

My breath came in fast pants, and I couldn't find the energy to close my legs, let alone anything else. The Fae around me took one look at my form and let out a humming laugh full of male satisfaction.

"Now that, I will remember," I murmured as my eyes slid closed and I fell asleep.

CHAPTER

I DIDN'T KNOW WHAT woke me. I bolted up from the ground, my heart racing and my eyes wide. I glanced around me and took in the sight of the Fae curled up next to me.

The twins lay next to each other on my left, one arm thrown over the other as if, even in their sleep, they couldn't bear to be apart. I smiled slightly and moved my eyes to Cheshire curled against the back of Hatter, his long furry tail wrapped around them both. Hatter's arm lay beneath where I had been laying, his clothes back on and his jacket covering my front. He had his hat tipped over his face so that only his mouth showed. I had the urge to lean down and kiss him but refrained.

I had a job to do.

Slowly, I slipped out from between them. I almost left Hatter's jacket but then thought better of it. Sliding my arms into the sleeves of it, I brought the arm up to my nose inhaling deeply. Letting out a quiet sigh, I searched for my shoes. I didn't bother looking for my drawers. Those had been destroyed and were a lost cause.

Giving the four of them one last lingering look, I tiptoed out of the garden and into the hedge maze. I moved cautiously, careful to remember the way the prince had led me before. The stars above were the only light to guide my way, and I forced myself to be brave.

"You can do this, Alice," I murmured to myself. "Just a bit further."

Every sound and snap of the branches beneath my feet made me jump until my footsteps increased. I was practically running by the time I reached the Orchard. My breathing came in pants, and I almost collapsed on the ground in my relief.

Pushing myself to keep going, I raced toward the door the prince had shown me before. When I arrived, I fingered the key in my pocket. I could leave now. I had practically said my goodbyes already. I could go home, tell my family goodbye, and then...

What? I could come back, but then I would age so quickly that I wouldn't be able to enjoy my time with the others. A blink of time and I would be gone, leaving them behind still gorgeous and thriving. They'd forget me of course. They've lived for centuries while I barely had twenty years on me.

A whisper made my head jerk to the side. "Girl."

I cocked my head to the side and squinted in the dark. "Hello? Is someone there?" I inched toward the bushes where the voice had come from. The whisper didn't sound again. However, when I reached to push back the branches of the bush, a light jumped out at me.

I hopped backward, my hand on my chest. "Watch!"

The opalaught held a lantern up between us, an annoyed expression on his face. "You're late, Ms. Liddell. Come, this way."

I didn't have the chance to ask him what I was late for before he raced back into the bushes, his light bobbing beside him.

"Wait," I called out, kneeling on the ground to follow him. I winced as a branch scraped my cheek. I pushed through the bushes, searching for the opalaught. Crawling into the opening I made, I found there was more behind them than the wall led me to believe. A faded sign sat to one side that I couldn't read in the dark. I pushed through the opening and shoved the vines and leaves out of my face. The light bounced around in front of me, leading me further and further into the hole I was now in.

"Watch!" I cried out and wiggled out of the hole and into a large circular alcove. Watch sat at the base of a giant tree adorned with glowing orange fruit. He wiggled his nose and tapped his watch before waving me closer.

"Where are we?"

"Finally, my apologies for the delay." Watch ignored me and appeared to be talking to the tree. He gave me one more disapproving look before hopping back toward the hole. "Well, I'll be off. Goodbye, Ms. Liddell."

Spinning around, I raced after him. "Hold on one darn minute. I have questions for you." I tried to follow him, but this time, the hole had grown too small for me to enter. With a huff and a stomp of my foot, I spun back around to the tree.

Staring up at it like it would talk to me, I waited. What was I supposed to do now? It felt like everything had been leading me to this place, to this very moment, but why?

I moved further into the clearing, looking for another way out but only seeing rocks and fallen fruit. The fruit on the ground had lost their brilliance, no inner light shone from the center. They were rotten and lifeless. The others, though, called to me.

I wondered what they tasted like. Their shape was like that of a peach, and when I pulled one from its branches, its skin felt like one. Unlike a peach, it warmed in my palm, and I was surprised to see the light inside of it didn't die out when I plucked it.

Bringing the fruit to my mouth, I bit into it. Juices filled my mouth and my eyes closed. A voice whispered in my mind. An ancient voice asking me what I desired more than anything in this world. I knew what I wanted without having to think about it. Thoughts of what the shadows had offered me, to be Fae, rushed to the forefront of my mind.

With each bite I took, the world around me changed. The juice of the fruit which had been a pleasantly sweet flavor became more prominent. I could taste every aspect of its existence, feel the different ridges of the skin of the fruit, smell the ground beneath my feet and the lingering scent of the opalaught, musky and wet.

My knees buckled beneath me, and I dropped the fruit. On my hands and knees much like I had been just hours ago, I gasped for air. My lungs burned, and my skin tingled. Every inch of me felt like it was being pulled at its seamed and restitched into a different design. I pinched my eyes closed tightly, moaning and praying the feeling to go away. I didn't want to die. Not yet. Not now.

It seemed like forever before I was finally able to breathe normally again. Shifting on the ground, I slowly opened my eyes. The dirt, I could see it, every single grain of dirt, rocks, and bugs wriggling beneath the ground. The smell of it assaulted my nose, earthy and moist. I turned my face from it and instantly regretted it.

Before Hatter's jacket had a pleasant aroma that made me warm and protected. Now, though it burned my nose, and I just wanted it off me. Before I had a chance to take the jacket off, my clothes morphed beneath my hands. The jacket shortened and changed from purple to a dark blue. My skirt lengthened and flared out, my drawers replaced with those I'd worn at home. Even the shoes on my feet changed. Little fingerless gloves covered my hands as I stared with awe.

My hands reached up to my head where my hair had been adjusted back into the lovely updo Coby had given me before, the little hat still sitting on my head. Was I Fae? Was this it?

I tried to make a cup of tea appear. Nothing. However, I was able to make my gloves change from pink to blue and then back. Interesting. I played with my powers, astonished to find out that I not only could change my clothes but my appearance. I made myself tall like my sister Rhoda and then short as Mop.

Giggling in glee, I spun around in place. This was better than I had ever hoped for. I could really use this.

I had a dark thought, a thought I would have never thought to have before this very moment. Chewing on my lower lip, I darted a look at the tree as if it could read my thoughts and then shook my head. I was being silly. It's just a tree.

Turning away from it, I flounced back to the hole which, at my approach, expanded and became a full entrance. I waltzed right through it and back into the Orchard, a merry little skip in my step. When I saw the door, my eyes brightened. My hand darted into my pocket, and I pulled out the key.

Not letting myself think about it, I shoved the key into the door and turned it. Pulling the door open, I peered inside before glancing back at the Orchard. I'd be back. I had one last thing to take care of.

CHAPTER

WHEN I CAME BACK through the doorway, I was beside myself. I couldn't stop thinking about the look on Lewis's face when I appeared in his bedroom.

"Alice! Where have you been?" he climbed out of his bed and reached for me. "I've been worried sick."

I shoved him away from me and snapped, "Were you? Were you really? Or were you upset that you lost your little storyteller?"

Lewis's brows furrowed. "Whatever do you mean? You ran away in the middle of our wedding."

"And I'm glad I did, or I would have found out I had been settling. Settling for this life." I threw my hands up around me and sneered. "And settling for you." I urged my magic forward and felt myself transforming before him, making his eyes widened and terror leak from his every pour. "I'll never let someone like you use me ever again."

Blinking back the memories, I grinned and raced for the edge of the Orchard. I couldn't wait to tell the others what had happened. How I didn't have to leave now. I could stay with them.

"Fae suits you."

I stumbled to a stop, falling backward and away from the collective voice, I had convinced myself had been a dream. There, hiding between the trees, they blinked at me. Large bulbous eyes covering a formless figure. Climbing back to my feet, I straightened my spine and faced them.

"Thank you. I am quite enjoying myself."

"We would hope so for the price it will cost you." They laughed, the sound of it burning my ears. "You have not forgotten our deal, have you?"

"No. I haven't," I growled, crossing my arms over my chest. "Go on. Tell me what you want in return, so I can get back."

"Oh, don't be too hasty. The payment time has come, and we are here to collect." They paused for dramatic effect and then continued, "The opalaught who helped you will help you again. Find the prince and make the princess feel something, or we'll make you and yours feel worse."

With those parting words, the shadows merged with the darkness around them leaving me befuddled and tired. Why couldn't they speak plainly? Why did it all have to be games and riddles? If there were one thing I would miss about humans, it was their blatant need to talk about everything.

I sat on the hill and thought, trying to piece together the puzzle pieces of the job the shadows had given me. As dawn began to approach, I had finally figured out something that I could use.

The shadows clearly wanted me to move the two royals in the right direction. Why they wanted the two of them to have a happily ever after when everyone else had claimed the shadows were bad made the whole situation confounding. However, I had gotten my part of the deal and had to play my part even if I didn't understand it.

The princess found me threatening. So, I could play with that. Jealousy could be a strong motivator.

The bright rising of the sun made me wince and blink my eyes against it. My new heightened senses were going to take some getting used to. My ears were still ringing from suddenly being able to hear everything.

Like the crunch of footsteps coming my way. I would never have been able to hear them had I still been human. Cheshire's steps were far lighter than anyone's I'd ever heard before, so being able to hear it at all was pure magic.

"What are you doing here?" I frowned, crossing my arms over my chest. "I thought you were sleeping?"

Cheshire arched a brow. "You aren't as quiet as you think you are, kitten." He shifted to my side, his tail falling from his shoulder and looping around my waist. "What are you doing up this early? You found some new clothes."

"Um, yes. The queen gave them to me." I gave him a weak smile as my mind blanked for any further explanation. I couldn't gather my thoughts quickly enough to come up with an excuse. I couldn't tell him I was waiting for the prince. I didn't want him to get the wrong idea, let alone know what I was planning to do.

"Uh, I needed a few moments alone." I clucked my tongue and then pointed toward the sunrise. "I wanted to see if the sunrise was the same here as back home."

"Understandable." Cheshire brushed his fingers along my jawline, and I shivered in pleasure. One good thing about the new senses, not only were eyes and ears enhanced, but every touch felt like a million strokes deep within me. "Why don't you come back to bed, and I'll show you the true pleasures of being with a Fae?"

I caught sight of Watch out of the corner of my eye. "Why don't you go, wake Hatter, and I'll come to join you in a moment? I wanted a word with Watch about sending my family a message."

Cheshire glanced to the opalaught and then back to me, his lips turning down in a frown. "Alright, but don't keep me waiting too long or Hatter will get impatient." He brushed his lips against my cheek before unwinding his tail from my waist, but not before he slid that tail between my things with a wicked grin.

Digging my nails into my hands, I smiled back. When he was out of sight, and Watch had entered the Orchard, I rushed to his side. "Watch, you need to get the prince right now."

"I would be happy to get your prince for you, what is the problem?" Watch adjusted his waistcoat and pulled a long chain out of his pocket, looking at the time. "There are but a few moments before dawn. Surely it can wait?"

"No." I shook my head. "It has to be now. There's a problem with the princess. She needed to see him, right now. It's a matter of life and death. The wedding depends on it."

Watch's face tensed, his furry brow raising in alarm. "Why didn't you say so in the first place? I will call for him at once."

"Thank you." I waved him off with a ragged breath. If I couldn't get the prince here, then the whole plan would go out of control. This had to work. The shadows had already helped me. If I didn't do my part, I didn't want to think about what they might do to me or even to the men in my life.

I feared more for them than about losing my powers. When they'd first offered me the deal, I didn't think it would be a big ordeal. Get some powers, cause a bit of drama, and everyone would go home happy, me in the arms of three handsome men. Now I'd be lucky if I'd get out of the whole thing with my head.

Dawn was approaching fast. I had better change my appearance before the prince arrived.

Closing my eyes, I took a deep breath. The magic inside of me was still new to me, and though it came when I called, it was sluggish. I thought about the Seelie Princess. Her long white blonde hair, her icy blue eyes so much like her mother's, and the pale blue form-clinging dress I'd seen her in last.

I'd only just finished the final touches and moved over to one of the largest trees in the Orchard when the prince appeared at the bottom of the hill. I forced myself to breathe slowly as he moved toward me. He looked so happy. So, thrilled to see me.

Fuck. I couldn't do this. I couldn't trick him.

But what about the shadows? I didn't want to go back to the human realm and leave all of this behind. Especially, since I had already ruined my former life with what I did to Lewis.

Guilt ate at me for deceiving him, but I pushed it down as he reached for me.

"Hello, my prince." I smiled at him, peering up at him from beneath my lashes. I hoped he didn't notice my change in behavior. I'd only met the princess a few times, I didn't know her well enough to know if she would be shy or hang all over him. I choose the safest route.

"Hello, my peach," he purred, sliding his hands down my back and cupping my backside.

I let out a surprised sound but didn't pull away. Well, it looks like I was wrong. Those two were just as bad as Cheshire and me.

His brows furrowed, and I forced myself to relax. "What's wrong? You act like I've never touched you before."

Oh, no. He was on to me. I have to act more like the princess.

"Nothing, nothing. Just wasn't expecting such a warm welcome is all." I gave him a shaky smile, hoping that it would be passed off as nerves and nothing else.

"Well, we are getting married tomorrow. I would hope that all of my welcomes are like this." He stroked a thumb across my face, searching for something that I prayed he didn't see.

"I'm sure they will be." I ducked my head and forced a blush to my cheeks.

"You are not having doubts now, are you?" He pulled back slightly, concern coloring his voice. "If there is something I have done, please tell me, and I will remedy it right now."

I swallowed and shook my head. "No, no." I pulled my lower lip into my mouth, chewing on it to keep myself from talking too much.

"Then what is it?" he urged me to tell him what was bothering me.

Offering him a soft smile, I murmured, "I just wanted to see you is all. I missed you."

Rain began to fall between the leaves of the tree, sprinkling us with water. I blinked rapidly against the falling water. It hadn't rained at all during the entire time I'd been here. Why would it choose to start now?

Pushing away the thought, I turned my attention back to the prince as he cupped my face with his hand. "I have missed you as well." Without warning, he swooped down and claimed my lips.

My fingers curled into the front of his shirt, and I tried to picture that I was kissing one of the others and not the prince. He wrapped his arms around me tighter, shoving his tongue into my mouth. Our tongue moved against each other for a moment, and then he froze.

Something was wrong. I knew I shouldn't have kissed him with tongue. Even with my new enhanced senses, I knew the difference between each of my men's taste. Why I thought it would be different with the prince, I didn't know.

A gasp from behind us caused the prince to rip his mouth away from mine. My heart pounded in my chest, and the guilt that rolled around in my stomach shot to my throat. The princess had seen us, and not only that, but the prince had seen the princess which meant in a few seconds, he would figure out it wasn't the princess he'd been kissing.

In my panic, I lost control of my glamour and could feel the change come over me just as the prince turned his questioning gaze back to me. Taking in my changed form, his face went through a series of emotions, from shock to disbelief and horror.

I smiled nervously at him, letting out a little giggle.

"What have you done?" he hissed, grabbing my shoulders.

"Just a bit of fun is all." I shrugged and tried to laugh it off.

The prince did not share my laughter and only seemed to become more enraged. His eyes darted toward the way the princess had disappeared and then back to me.

"I will deal with you later," he snarled before running down the hill after the princess.

The rain was coming down harder now, as if the Underground knew the princess and prince were upset. I hoped this would push them in the right direction. That I hadn't lied and made a fool of myself of nothing.

I lifted my skirt and raced through the Orchard, not caring that I was getting wet in my hurry. I couldn't find the prince or the princess, and I'd already gotten to the end of the line. Then something made my feet start toward the hidden alcove the tree I'd gotten my powers from lived in.

Hurrying into the alcove, I stopped at the entrance. The princess was no where to be found but the prince stood at the bottom of the tree. He screamed and hit the tree. He pounded on the roots, screaming for them to give her back.

Give who back? Where was the princess? Did the tree kill her?

A small gasp snuck out and my hand came up to my mouth as I realized what I had done. Oh, my Lord. This was all my fault. Who'd known a little kiss would cause so much trouble? I was just trying to help. They told me I was helping them.

"Your Highness?" I called out, and he stopped attacking the tree. Turning around, his eyes landed on me, and I froze in place. He stalked toward me his hands dripping with blood.

Tears fell down my face, and I reached for him. "I was only trying to help. The shadows said I could be one of you and I am. Look." I held a hand out to show him my powers, but he didn't even bother to look.

"I'm quite aware of your newfound abilities, Alice." He cursed so loudly that I cringed. "Did you think for a moment that the shadows could have lied? That they

231

would tell you anything you wanted to hear? Just so you would do what they wanted?"

My heart pounded in my chest as I scrambled for an explanation something to help defuse the situation. "But why would the shadows want to keep you apart? Surely they couldn't care less about your marriage?"

"You couldn't be more wrong." His laugh was bitter and heavy, making me feel even worse. "They have as much invested in my marriage as I do, except I had more to lose."

"Why? What do they gain from breaking you two up?" I cocked and tried to understand what had happened. How could I have been so easily doped?

"That's the question, isn't it?" he snarled, not looking at me any longer.

The prince wouldn't tell me more, but he didn't need to. I knew I'd messed up. I'd been tricked by those shadows. Sure, I'd gotten what I wanted but what they wanted had been even worse. Who knew what the cost of my mistake would bring?

The sound of pounding feet coming toward us made my sobs come in harder. "I'm sorry. I'm so sorry. I didn't mean it."

But it was too late now.

"And you will have plenty of time to think about the answer. Guards!" his voice rose, and the walls shook around us. "Everything that happens from here on out is on your shoulders."

I crumbled onto the ground, realizing that everything had been for nothing. I'd gone through the whole ordeal to become Fae to be with the men I loved, and now I would never see them again. Two hands grabbed beneath my arms and hauled me to my feet. I didn't even try to fight them, knowing it wouldn't do any good. I might be a Fae now, but I had only been magical for a day. They'd been magical all their lives. There was no way I'd ever beat them.

Somehow, the whole of the Underground knew something was going on because the Orchard, which had been empty before, was now filled to the brim with people. They were gathering around the alcove where the guards dragged me out. Each whisper and jeer was like a knife through my heart. I thought there was no way I'd ever feel more humiliated than that very moment.

Until I saw four faces I never thought I'd see again. The guards were keeping them back as the twins fought against them to get to me. Cheshire glared at me, his fangs baring as I passed by.

Hatter reached out and almost touched me. Thanks to my new powers, I could barely hear the words he was calling out to me over the crowd, "Alice dear, what have you done?"

I shook my head and pinched my eyes shut not wanting to see the disappointment and anger on their faces. I wanted to remember them the way they were before I messed it all up, happy and content around the picnic we'd had in the garden. If I'd know it would be our last joyful moment, I'd have savored it more. Now, it was too late.

CHAPTER

THE RESOUNDING SOUND OF the iron door slamming shut behind me would haunt me for several decades. It would become the one sound that would always link me back to my cell. I presumed all prisoners felt the same way at some point.

My eyes scanned around the gray stone walls, the bare floors, and the single window on the opposite side of the room. Did Fae not have regular bodily functions? Did they not need to sleep or eat? All of these questions ran through my mind as I stood in the middle of my prison cell, questions I never took the time to ask before I ruined my life. My now eternal life.

"Well, I supposed that was a plus," I spoke out loud, and the words echoed back to me, making me frown, "and a negative." An eternity by myself in a room with nothing had to be worse than death.

Panic crept through my chest, causing my heart to bang against my ribs. I spun around the room and raced toward the door. My hands reached up to bang against it. However, before my fingers even touched the surface, a searing heat flared across my skin. I yelped, jerking my arms back. A frustrated growl ripped through me, and I spun on my heels. My eyes landed on the window. The singular decorative item in the room was covered in an ornate gold frame that looked out of place in the dull gray walls. Racing over to the window, I pushed my face against the glass.

"Hello?" I shouted, not able to see past the dark red nothing. It seemed as if something covered the window. If I turned my head just so, I could almost make out more stone walls and even what might have been another window covered in the same material. I tried to call out once more, screaming and shouting until my throat burned and my eyes swelled from crying.

Finally, when my spirit had all but exhausted, I turned around, placing my back against the wall and sinking down to the floor. What had I done? Was all of this worth it? No. If I could take it back, I would. I'd rather have had a few short human years with my beloveds than this lifetime of solitude. I'd go mad here on my own without anything to keep my mind off the guilt and the hatred of what I had done.

I wiped my face on my dress, blowing my nose on the skirt. Pulling back, I grimaced at the mess I'd made. I reached for the new abilities I'd acquired and attempted to manifest a new gown. Nothing happened. I tried again. Still nothing. My brow furrowed, and I pushed until my head ached, but still my gown stubbornly stayed dirty and stained.

"So, not only am I going to be deprived of anything humane, but the powers I'd given up everything to receive were gone as well." I sighed and banged my head against the wall. "Fuck." The word still felt foreign in my mouth, but I had nothing and no one to impress. No one to tell me I was being improper or even to blush adorably in front of at the sound. I was utterly alone.

At some point, I slept.

I dreamed of being offered the same deal before, but this time, I told them no. That in no way would I betray my prince. I was happy to be human. The dream turned cold, the shadows closing in on me, making me shiver and quake. My eyes jolted open.

The hard floor I had fallen asleep on had turned soft and smelled faintly of lavender. My eyes fell on the bed beneath my body and trailed over the now not-so-empty cell. A bookshelf sat at the opposite side of the room, filled to the brim with more books than I could ever imagine reading in my lifetime. Well, my human lifetime. A desk sat beneath the window, but before I could check to see what else might be different about my cell, a slithering, whispering sound came from outside of my cell.

I scrambled off the bed, toward the door, and started to open my mouth to shout but stopped. Something was wrong. My eyes blinked at the wall, and while my powers might not be working, my heightened senses still were alive and well. There was a dark aura, corrupted, and so volatile it made me gag.

I swallowed hard, forcing myself to breathe through my nose. Whatever was on the other side of that door was not something I wanted to pay attention to me.

Just as I resigned myself to crawl into my new bed, a tugging sensation came over me. Frozen in place, my breathing quickened. The only way I could describe the feeling coming over me was like a claw had dug into my chest and squeezed around my heart. I couldn't fight, I couldn't even scream. All I could do was stand there and let it take what it wanted from me. And take it did.

My energy seeped out, and with it, my memories. I could just barely grab onto them, peeking at what was being taken from me, and a single tear slid down my face. The last night I had with all my beloveds together. Cheshire's face as he quietly sat by, watching the twins squabble over who would get to sit next to me. Hatter stroking my hair, muttering lovely words, plans for our future. As quickly as I saw the image, it was gone, I couldn't bring it back to my mind, and then after a moment, I didn't even know what I was trying to remember at all.

The darkness left then, slithering down the hallway I knew resided outside my cell door, no doubt to feed on some other poor soul trapped in the Seelie Queen's prison. I collapsed to the floor, taking a moment to mourn for my lost memory, before standing. I threw myself down on the bed and gripped the single blanket, wrapping it around me. I squeezed my eyes shut, wishing away what had happened and knowing there was no one there to grant any more wishes.

Years past or so I thought. It must have. I slept. I woke up. I read books. I cried. Then I slept again. No food was brought, but then

239

again, I never became hungry. My questions were answered each day that I didn't die or feel the need to daily necessities a human would require.

Eventually, I became used to my singular existence. The only companions I had were the books that seemed to populate on their own and the darkness. The darkness was a constant terror keeping me in perpetual fear. Fear of what memory I'd lose. Fear of it finally feeding on the last of me. Fear of it never ending.

It was always the same. Until one day, it wasn't.

There were voices outside my window. Not the usual shuffling of feet as the guards or whoever the queen had patrolling, but voices of people who weren't supposed to be there.

"Hey! How do you know my full name?" a female voice accused their companion.

I dropped the book I had been reading and jumped up. Racing to the window, I shoved my face against the glass. My ear strained to hear what they were saying, as if whoever had come might be able to help me.

"I know quite a many things." He paused and then the footsteps continued toward me. "Not all of them pleasant, though if you didn't want anyone to know, you shouldn't talk to yourself like no one is listening. Someone is always listening." I jerked back for a moment, wondering if he knew I was listening. "Now, if you are finished wasting time, I can hear the guards moving around above." He paused once more. I sagged, realizing it wasn't me that he was worried about. "More than likely getting ready to remove that pretty little head of yours."

This was my chance. This was my moment. If there were ever a time, I would get free this would be it. "Hello? Is anyone there?" My voice sounded like I had swallowed a bucket of frogs. Of course, I hadn't used it in years. There was no need, not unless I wanted to talk to myself.

Something moved behind the red material. The form hesitated and turned its head one way and then the other as if listening for my voice. The other person tapped itself foot, no doubt impatient for their companion to get moving.

"Hello?" I called out again, hoping they would come to my window.

The figure, who I could now tell was a woman, moved toward my window. Her brow furrowed, and her lips pursed into a tight frown. She stared into my cloth covered window, and her hand reached up to grab the fabric. I wished with all my might that she might pull it off. That I might see

241

something anyone else besides the four walls of my cell.

"You don't want to be doing that, Lady." The other voice was a smooth, crooning type straight out of my books. The owner, I imagined, would be just as attractive as the writers portrayed.

"Who's that?" the woman asked, and I frowned. Were they just going to stand there and argue over me?

"No one of importance," the male voice huffed, placing himself between the frame and the woman.

"Then why does it matter if I see or not?" She tried to glance around his shoulder as if she could see into my window through the material.

Fed up with being ignored, I called out trying my best to sound helpless. "Is anybody there? It's so lonely in here. Please help me." Surely, they would help me now? Who would leave a poor girl all alone in a cell by their selves?

The Seelie Queen did, a voice in my head reminded me.

Well, besides her.

"Chess," the woman spoke to the man, a sharpness to her tone, "I'm not leaving this spot until I see what is in there."

"Believe me, Lady," he tried to direct the woman, Lady, away from my window, "anyone who is in there deserves it."

"Like I deserved to lose my head?"

I nodded tightly. Too true.

"This..." the man, Chess, what an unusual name, explained, "... is the Hall of Mirrors. This is where all the very naughty Fae are kept."

I huffed. Well, I never. I might have made one mistake, but that didn't make me naughty.

"Oh." Lady sounded dejected, and I knew I was losing her. I had to do something anything to get her to pull the material off the mirror. I had to get out of here.

When they started to move away, I cried out the only thing I could think of, "But I'm not a Fae! I'm human!"

"What?" Lady jerked away from Chess. He cursed and tried to grab her.

It was too late. She had already gotten a hold of the material and was yanking it free. The red cloth fell away and revealed a woman I'd never seen before.

Red hair possibly messier than my own covered the head of a curious looking woman. Forest green eyes surveyed me with interest, and then they opened wide, her mouth falling open. The man next to her seemed familiar to me with his pale pink locks and bright green eyes, but I couldn't place him. The scowl on his face was familiar enough, I'd seen something similar in my dreams, and a fond feeling swelled in my chest, but I couldn't quite grab the reason why. I added it to one of the many memories the darkness had stolen from me.

However, my lost memories were not as important as the woman in front of me, who had gotten over her initial shock. Her mouth opened and closed like a fish, and a single word fell from her lips.

"Alice," she breathed out.

I only had a moment to wonder how she knew my name and then realized it wasn't important as long as I could get out of my prison cell. Hope swelled inside of me. The hope that my long sentence would soon be over. That I might finally see someone outside of my cell. That maybe, just maybe, I might see Hatter.

"Yes, that's my name. Alice Liddell."

Author Note

I know! Don't hate me. There is more to come I promise.

Alice will return in her own full-length series soon but while you wait find out what happened next for Alice in the completed series following the mysterious saviors in Chasing Rabbits!

Check out the first chapter on the next page.

Don't stop there! You can check out the full love story between the prince and princess of the Underground in the novella, Chasing Hearts!

Chapter 1

THE CHASE

BRANDI BRIDGERS WAS a bitch in high school, and as I watched her sitting behind her desk with her 'holier-than-thou' attitude and her stylishly bobbed blonde hair, she gave me little hope she had changed. I rolled my eyes as she adjusted her neck-high white blouse. Her lips pressed together in a thin line as she scanned over my credentials. My resume dangled in her hand like it was something she found at the bottom of her drain.

"...come home."

My eyes widened, snapping up to look at Brandi. "What did you say?"

Brandi's lips tilted in a frown at my question. "I said, I'm not surprised you came home after all this time. Almost everyone comes home eventually. Really, Katherine, this is an interview, you really should be paying more attention."

"Sorry," I grumbled, too fixated on what I thought I'd heard. *Come home.* The words had plagued me for over a year now.

It started shortly after my twenty-first birthday. At first it was a whisper in a dream that I'd brushed off as being homesick, but then it bled into my waking life. I'd hear it in the breeze, or in my economics class. One time I swore my own reflection said it back to me. I had also been drunk out of my mind at the time, but it was hard to believe they were all coincidences.

So, here I was, back in my hometown, and the words were still taunting me. I was home. I couldn't get any more home than Iowa. I was even looking for a job. Not that I had high hopes for this interview, but with an English Literature Degree, there weren't many options available. I learned that painful truth back in New York; I should have been an accountant.

"I see here you were a library assistant in high school." Brandi's voice had a high-pitched, 'bless-your-heart' tone to it that grated on my nerves.

"Yes, Brandi. We went to high school together, you already know that." I crossed my arms over my black silk blouse, careful not to catch my thick copper hair on the buttons of my sleeves. My choice to wear a

247

black shirt over a white one, like my mother had suggested helped to keep me from jumping over the desk to wring her grace's little neck. I didn't want to match Brandi in any way, shape, or form.

Brandi's brown eyes peeked around the side of the piece of paper, which held my meager life experience, bare to her over-accentuated eyes. "Katherine, as I told you before, I won't let our history together affect my judgment. No matter how offensive." She sniffed as her gaze returned to the paper as if her thinly veiled reference to my previous transgressions didn't affect her.

Like I had ever given two shits about what she thought.

Years ago, when I was an angry teen rebel full of sarcasm and black nail polish, I had the displeasure of going to school with Brandi and her swarm of over-medicated vultures. While everyone else in our class was trying to make as many memories as possible, I had spent the majority of it applying to every coast school I could afford. No place was far enough away from them.

So, when the miraculous day came and I got my acceptance letter to New York University, I didn't waste any time with long goodbyes. I gave Iowa a middle finger salute and made my way out of town screaming 'fuck you' to every innocent bystander I saw on my way down Broadway.

I probably should have been more selective of my targets, but how was I to know I would be sitting in an interview with one of the few people who actually deserved it?

My eyes narrowed at my captor, and I growled out, "Kat."

"What?" Brandi did not offer me her eyes this time.

"I like to be called Kat, which you also know."

For more than the first time – hell it was more like the hundredth time – I regretted coming to the interview. I would have turned tail and ran the moment I saw her, but my mother had gotten me the interview. If I left without even giving myself the chance to fail, I would never hear the end of it. I had to sit and swallow the half-assed insults to my person and abilities and hope to whatever deity was listening that I didn't get the job.

"Of course." Her voice still held a sickly sweet tone. "I'll make a note of it in your file." Her neatly manicured fingers gripped her pen as she scribbled onto a notepad.

I doubted she was actually making a note of it. It was probably a reminder to get her roots bleached again, or to tell the vultures about how Katherine Nottington had sloppily begged for a job. I am sure they would all have a good laugh over their next mani-pedi excursion.

"Well." She gave an exaggerated sigh. "You don't really have the qualifications we are looking for in a librarian. An English Literature degree is all fine and dandy, but you never learned the Dewey Decimal System."

"I completely understand, I will just–" I stood up, happy for the interview to finally be over.

"But." Her tone stopped me. "Your mother is a good friend of ours, and she contributes quite a bit to the funding of this town's community. It would be rash, not to mention unchristian like, to toss you out into the cold when you have been brave enough to come back to our – what was it you called this town?" She paused, pretending as if it were not on the tip of her tongue. "A prehistoric cesspool that didn't deserve the pavement it was built on?"

Why could she remember a nonsensical insult stated under the influence, but she couldn't remember I liked being called Kat?

My brow furrowed at her words. "So, I got the job?"

"You've got the job!" Brandi threw her hands up as she hopped out of her seat and enveloped me in a tight embrace.

My body tensed at the sudden intrusion to my personal space. She dwarfed me in her three-inch heels. My nose went smack to the middle of her neck where it was assaulted by her top-shelf perfume.

I had gotten the job. How the hell had that happened? I hadn't been pleasant. Hell, I had been snarky at best. I knew she didn't want me on her staff any more than I wanted to be there, but money talked, and if there is one thing my family had going for them it was money.

"Yay." I gave a small, half-hearted response.

"Let me introduce you to our team!" Brandi finally let me go and led me out to the main circulation desk where the other employees were waiting.

The 'team,' as she called it, consisted of two people. Two. And they seemed to have as much enthusiasm for Brandi's leadership as I did in being there. Yay just about covered it.

"This is David." Brandi pointed at a guy about my age who gave me a shy smile and then a nervous cough at Brandi's overshadowing presence. "He does most of the shelving, but he also works the desk with Mrs. Jenkins here."

Mrs. Jenkins was an elderly lady. She had dark-brown skin that contrasted nicely with the whitest hair I had ever seen. That kind of white hair wasn't seen in the city if it didn't come out of a box or a salon. I must have been staring, because the old woman's eyes narrowed into a glare.

"You got a problem?" Her voice was raspy as if she had smoked too much.

"Only on days that end with y." I gave a half smile at my own joke, and then frowned when her brow furrowed further before she barked out a laugh causing David and Brandi to jump.

"That's nice. I think we are going to get along just fine." She turned a sharp eye to Brandi. "I half expected another one of those prissy little chits you keep hiring." She glanced over at me with a crooked smile. "Couldn't stand them, with all their 'rules are rules' nonsense. Bah. Brandi here knows what's what."

"Yes, well," Brandi began, she seemed nervous with Mrs. Jenkins's attention on her. "We decided to take a chance and go a different direction this time."

The fact that the old lady ruffled Miss Prim and Proper's feathers made me instantly like her. At least someone in this place had a sense of humor. I needed some humor in my life.

Come home, the voice had said. I was home. So why was I still feeling like I had somewhere to be?

* * *

A WEEK LATER and nothing extraordinary had happened. I went about my mediocre life and the ever-present words that followed me were deafeningly silent. I was afraid to let my guard down, not that my mother would let that happen.

I found myself having my usual argument with my mother over my social life, or rather, the lack of a social life, of which I had become so proud. We had already gone over everything new in her life, so of course she had to start in on mine. My hands were busy washing dishes with anal-retentive detail as my mother harped in my ear.

"Katherine, I just don't understand why you won't at least have dinner with Kevin. He's a nice boy, and he has a job!" My mother's exasperated voice grated on my ear as I held my cell phone between my shoulder and face.

"Because, Mom, I don't want or need a boyfriend. I am fine on my own."

I surveyed the dish I was cleaning, making sure all the food had been rinsed off before putting it in the dishwasher. Nothing got on my nerves more than food stuck to a plate, but at the moment, my mother was riding in at a close second.

"Oh, yes, a twenty-two-year-old woman all alone in that big house— in the middle of nowhere—is completely fine."

I rolled my eyes at the sarcasm in her voice.

"It's Iowa, Mom. The whole state is practically in the middle of nowhere." I shoved the sleeves of my gray, NYU sweatshirt back up over my elbows and switched the phone to my other shoulder. "Besides, Crescent is only a few minutes outside of town and Grandma needs someone to take care of her house while she's off playing in Florida."

"And she told you you could sell it and put it toward a house in town. There is nothing wrong with wanting to be independent, Katherine, but being a hermit is drawing the line. Isn't being a librarian seclusion enough for you?"

A snort left my nose before I could stop it. The fact that she disapproved of the very job she pulled strings to get me was astounding. Though, it shouldn't have been surprising, she was always the one who brought up her disapproval of my career choices.

She had been one of the ones who had griped at me to pick a sensible major, like accounting or, God forbid, political science. She never understood my love for the English language. I wanted to be an editor, or maybe even a writer. If I could ever buckle down and write something worth reading.

Lately, though, it seemed like I couldn't do anything right. This was probably due to my sister, Linda, also known as Miss Fucking Perfect, who was getting married this month. My mom had it in her head that I needed to find a man and be more social, or I would be doomed to be an old maid by thirty.

"You don't want to still be marking single when you're thirty do you?"

I should have bought a Powerball with how right I was.

There were worse things out there than being single at thirty. I could be dying of cancer or be a drug addict. No, my mother cared more about how my being single reflected on her.

"I'm not secluded at the library," I argued, ignoring her question completely. "Plenty of people are in and out every day. Plus, there are other workers there, not just me. Mrs. Jenkins works there, and so does David."

"Ha! Hardly suitable companionship for a girl your age. A senile old lady who has probably been there since the library opened, and David is more of a hermit than you! Though, if you dated him, at least you'd be dating. And Lord knows you'd never have to worry about him cheating on you. He hardly has the looks to be picky."

David was a nice guy, even if he was not the most attractive. He had a slightly hooked nose and a pudgy build, but after a week of working with him, I found his hesitant smile and soft-spoken ways endearing. If I was looking for someone, and I was not, he had a lot of the qualities I would want. Too bad he was taken.

"I'll make sure to tell his fiancé you think so."

I almost dropped the dish in my hand when she gave an uncharacteristic chortle. "Even that spud has someone! Doesn't that tell you anything, Katherine?"

My knuckles turned white as I gripped the plate in my hands. It started to make a tiny cracking noise, and I put it down. My mother had that effect on me. We would start fighting and she would pick and pick at old wounds until they bled. Sadly, my dishes were always the ones to suffer.

I slammed the dishwasher closed as I took a deep breath. "You know what, Mom? If it will make you happy, I will go out with Kevin, but not this week." I waited for the comment that was sure to come because she wasn't getting her way.

"But if you don't go out this week, you won't have enough prep time to have him be your date to Linda's wedding."

Linda's wedding. Of course, that's what she was worried about. No way would it be about my happiness.

"I'm in the wedding, Mom. The groomsmen assigned to me will be my date." I yanked the hair tie from my copper locks and set to work on tying the messy bun again. "Besides, I'm busy this week."

"Oh? Busy with what? That old garden?" I could almost see her rolling her eyes even though we were on the phone. "You know nothing good ever grows in your grandmother's yard. I should know. I grew up there."

"Yes, the garden, and if you'd bother to come over you would see how great everything is growing. I even have a carrot patch–"

As if knowing I was talking about it, a loud crash came from the backyard signaling my trap had gone off again. Damn rabbits!

"I've got to go."

"But Katherine, what about–"

"I'll talk to you on Sunday at lunch. Love you, bye," I cut in hanging up the phone before she could answer. I dashed to the door, shoved my feet into my sneakers, and took off toward the sound.

I scanned the backyard for any sight of the little thief who had been plaguing me for weeks. I skipped going into the garden. I knew my trap would be empty like it always was and skimmed the trees for any sign of the white devil instead. My forest-green eyes caught sight of a white streak bolting for the woods behind the house. Not wanting to lose him, I took off into the dark.

"Where did you go?"

The green of the trees created a darkened gray, making it hard to see as they blended into their surroundings. The rustling leaves to my left drew my attention just as the dull white streak made for the clearing up ahead.

"There you are!"

My sneakers thudded against the ground as I chased after him, and the whispers returned. With each footfall they chanted. *Come home. Come home. Come home.* My heart beat faster in my chest and my bare legs seemed to catch on every single branch I ran past, leaving little scratches all over my skin.

I ignored the stinging in my legs and kept my eyes on the white coat that glared neon in the visible moonlight from the clearing. Though I had a clear view of him, he was still too fast for me to catch. I wasn't in the best of shape, and my short legs could only get me so far.

The wind picked up as I bent over to catch my breath. The words floated on the wind as it whipped bits of hair out of my bun and into my face. I glowered at the single section of blonde that had fallen, its contrast so different from the rest of my copper hair. A birthmark at the nape of my neck had caused the discoloration. I usually kept my hair down to hide it. The fact that I even let it show at home would cause my mother to start a tirade about how I should just color it.

I didn't really care about it, and probably should have given into her urgings, but I didn't see the logic in buying a box of hair color just for a single section. I wasn't so vain to think the expense was worth it, so it hung freely underneath my hair with none the wiser. Plus, it pissed my mother off, which was reason enough in my book.

Standing up, I noticed the rabbit had stopped next to the little pond my sister and I used to fish at when we were younger. It wasn't a very big pond, and to our dismay, it had more frogs than fish in it. It did have a great little hiding spot. There was a cave where water from the Missouri River trickled into the pond, and sitting right outside the cave, taking his time as he enjoyed my carrots, was the long-eared fiend.

He munched away at one with every confidence he had lost me. I took a moment to try to get the jump on him by moving across the field toward where he was sitting. Luck was not on my side, however, because as soon as I was about to sneak up behind him, he saw my reflection in the pool and panicked. He shoved the carrot into his mouth and darted toward the mouth of the cave.

"Shit."

The rabbit was more trouble than he was worth and a lot smarter than he seemed. I had tried everything to keep him out of my garden. Animal repellent, traps, even wire fencing. It still didn't keep him out. He had somehow even cut a hole in the fence big enough for him to get in and out with my carrots.

No clue how he pulled that one off.

I once mused he was a runaway lab rabbit that the government had been doing experiments on him. As a result, he'd become a superfied genius rabbit. Though, if that were true, nothing short of a high-powered security system was keeping that rabbit out of my carrot patch. So, since I couldn't afford that kind of tech on a librarian's salary, I decided to take him out.

In order to not spook my prey again, I inched my way toward the cave's entrance. It wasn't very big. At ten years old it had been quite easy to go in and out as I pleased, but as a moderately chested grown woman, it was a tight fit.

I tried to be as quiet as possible as I sucked in my stomach. Think thin. I was as thin as a rod, as skinny as a Victoria Secret model. This wasn't making me claustrophobic whatsoever. Finally, I got through the entrance and blinked as my eyes adjusted to the dim lighting in the cavern.

The cave I remembered was usually pretty dark with only a sliver of moonlight coming through the opening, but to my surprise, it was brighter in the cavern than it was outside. As my eyes adjusted to the cave an ominous feeling washed over me. Weird, neon-white painted symbols covered the walls.

What the hell?

My fingers traced one of the symbols, and I realized it was not paint at all. It was as if they were part of the wall itself. I didn't remember them being there the last time my sister and I had ventured into our little hideout. I would remember mysterious nightlights, wouldn't I?

As conspiracy theories started to circle my mind, a sneeze from the back of the cavern reminded me of my purpose. I turned away from the mysterious symbols and moved toward the sound. Every step I took felt heavier than the last, and a chilling thought came to mind—what if something, or someone, was in the cave?

With that disturbing thought, my footsteps became more cautious, and my eyes darted around. No one was going to get the jump on me. I had read enough horror novels to know I was a prime candidate for being abducted or killed by some lunatic with a skin fetish. I really should work on my sense of self-preservation.

More symbols started to appear on the walls the further back I got. In the front of the cavern they had only been on the sides, but as I progressed deeper into the cave, the symbols began to run all along the ceiling and the floor. They were angled in the direction of something in the center of the back of the cavern as if they were being drawn in.

I followed the spiral of symbols until I ended up in front of a basketball-sized hole in the wall. That had definitely not been there before. Turning around in a circle, I searched the walls for any other changes. There was not really anything different, besides the weird nightlights and the hole, and there was no sign of the rabbit anywhere.

I gave the hole a wide berth as I contemplated what to do next. I knew the only exit to the cavern was the one I came through, so the rabbit must have gone through the hole. Then again, I could be in a horrible version of some mummy story, and the moment I stuck my arm in that thing, it was going to get eaten off.

I wasn't the bravest person. I didn't agree to work in a library just because I loved to read, and I'd admit, a little desperate. It was quiet, making it easy to get lost in one's thoughts, which I was known to do on a semi-permanent basis. There also the seclusion from the lack of employees, which made it an anti-social's dream job.

Though, sometimes being so alone could have consequences, such as not being good with people, or more specifically, guys. I usually became either a stuttering mess or a sarcastic asshole when faced with an attractive specimen. That's why I liked working with David so much. He was plain enough I could be myself.

Mrs. Jenkins knew how I felt about men and people in general. She could be as bad as my mother when it came to me dating. I could just imagine what she would have to say about my hesitancy to stick my arm in that hole. "Dear, everything worth having comes with a leap of faith. Just hold onto your panties and take the plunge."

I had only been working at the library for a day when she said that to me. I had been so shocked; I had fallen out of my seat from laughing so hard. Yes, she was a little eccentric. She takes the whole 'I'm old so I can say whatever I want' a little too far, but she had a lot of great advice, and I already loved her for it.

I took a deep breath and let it out. "What the hell."

I stepped back up to the hole and placed one hand on each side of it. I bent at the waist and squinted into the hole to see what waited.

Darkness.

While the cavern was lit up with the glowing symbols, the hole was nothing but complete blackness. I couldn't see a damn thing. I blew out a shaky breath between my teeth, all that lead up and nothing.

"Fuck it."

I threw up my hands and moved away from the hole. That rabbit was not worth becoming some creepy crawlies food. Studying the symbols as I walked away, I made a mental note to dig into the language section when I got back to work in the morning.

"Does Mop think Lady is gone, does Mop?"

I turned an ear back toward the hole at the squeaky voice's question. I took large strides, well as large as my short legs would let me back to the hole.

Who was that?

"I don't know! Ye shouldn't have led her here in the first place!" A low rumbling voice growled in return.

I inched my face down to the hole and peered in again. Instead of darkness, there was a fading light coming from inside the hole. *Come home*, whispered against my face. I twisted around to look behind me. As usual, no one was there. Shoving down every part of me that screamed to just go back to the house and crawl into bed, I reached into the hole.

The warmth of the light engulfed my hand and tugged me toward it. I tried to retract my hand, but it was too late, it had its hooks in me. I remembered wondering if this is what it felt like to be sucked through a straw before everything went black.